79 UXBRIDGE ROAD

By Annette Creswell

Outer Banks Publishing Group
Raleigh/Outer Banks

FIRST EDITION – October 2022

Library of Congress Control Number: 2022945373

ISBN – 978-1-7367218-5-8
eISBN – 979-8-2010400-8-6

Dedicated to the Family

Acknowledgment

I wish to thank my wonderful agent Emerantia Parnall-Gilbert of Hawskspurr Productions for her friendship and invaluable assistance in bringing my novels to fruition.

My gratitude also extends to my publisher Anthony Policastro and all the dedicated team at Outer Banks Publishing Group.

Finally, a special thanks to Brett whose inspiration and encouragement resurrected my interest in writing.

Also by Annette Creswell

The Lodgers

When Mabel, a former Vaudeville performer, lands a job managing a boarding house on the ocean, she appears to attract a disparate cast of lodgers, all with unfortunate and dark lives.

The lodgers include:

Two queens, old thespian friends of Mabel's who live in the basement with a peppercorn rent.

Therese is a pregnant Irish girl banished to England by her mother who assumes she is in an unmarried mother's home in the care of the nuns.

Irene, a recovering alcoholic who has a sister

Judy, due to a trauma experienced during the war is unable to speak.

Arthur, an aged army major, had a son Ned who was shot for desertion.

Harry, alias Percy, a con man and felon who befriends the landlady,

Mabel. When Therese moves to the Outback to get married, Judy follows and one day Judy spots a Kookaburra in a nearby tree. When the bird laughs, an unexpected, wondrous miracle happens.

The DARK before the DAWN

Annette Creswell

The Dark Before the Dawn

Just before the start of World War II, Peggy Davis, a London midwife, has a chance encounter with a stranger that changes her life forever.

When Peggy meets Charles, a wealthy lord as she boards a bus in front of Harrods department store, fate casts them together.

When Charles' wife, Diana, and first child die in childbirth, Peggy, and Charles are thrust into a relationship of happiness, sorrow, and unexpected tragedy.

They ultimately marry, have a son, and adopt an east-end refugee boy from London.

What transpires is a web of family dramas a la Downton Abbey with lesbian relationships, Nazi sympathizers, and family secrets revealed as Peggy attempts to navigate through her new life from midwife to lady of the manor.

Chapter One

79 UXBRIDGE ROAD

For the Family

"Ma, ma," yelled Brian. "Can I play with my train?"

"Shoosh, keep your voice down, pet! You can only play for a while. I want you in the bath shortly and don't forget, it's hair washing night tonight."

Brian scuttled up the stairs to his room and shut the door. He wanted a bit of peace after a day at school where he was pushed over and it wasn't his fault, and he knew not to make too much noise as his father could not tolerate it.

Since his father had returned home from the war everything had changed. Either he spent most of the day in bed or sitting in his chair staring into space. He had a bad cough too. Mother said it was from the conditions in that camp in the war, and said his nerves were bad so everyone had to be quiet. Sometimes at night, Brian and his sister Janey would be woken up by his screams as he relived the horrors he had experienced.

His father was somewhat of a stranger to Brian, as he had been born when his father was fighting the Hun. He had heard his mother and the adults talk about these Hun, and what damage they had wrought on all the soldiers who had returned to Britain.

Whenever the neighbour from next door came over, there was a lot of whispering which led to Brian putting his ear to the keyhole to elicit some gossip.

His mother, when she caught him doing this, told him there was never anything good to be heard by eavesdropping and giving his ear a pinch for good measure!

"Brian," called his mother through the door "Your bath is ready. Hurry up now."

"Alright, I'm coming" replied Brian giving his train one last run around the track. He passed by Janey in the kitchen topping and tailing the beans for tea. He took a few and popped them into his mouth.

"Stop that Brian, these are for our tea and there aren't that many as it is. You know there's a shortage of food. Go and get in the bath for goodness sake, and make sure you scrub that dirty neck or there'll be hell to pay from ma."

He wandered into the sitting room where the fire was burning and, throwing off his clothes got into the tub. His father was sitting in his usual chair staring into the flames, the newspaper lying on his lap.

"Hello da" said Brian.

"Hello, son" replied his father. "Did you have a good day at school?"

"It was alright," said Brian sucking the end of the washer "Except Dudley took my ruler and when I tried to get it back he pushed me over."

"Did you give him a good thump?"

"No da, he's too big. Da, can you come with us to the party next Saturday?"

"What party?"

"You know, the party in the street. Everyone's going."

"I don't know son, I'll see how I feel, alright?"

"Alright, da."

"Now get a move on. Have you washed your neck properly?"

"That's what Janey said. Why does everyone go on about my neck?" he said as he flailed the washer around to the vicinity of his neck.

"And don't forget about those ears. You don't want to have turnips growing in them."

Just then his mother Martha came in.

"Brian, haven't you finished yet? Let me have the soap to wash your hair. I hope you haven't got any more lice."

She took the soap and lathered Brian's head then gave it a good scrub.

"Ouch, ma, that hurts!"

"Sorry, pet but I have to make sure it's clean. Now a good rinse off and you're done. At least Janey has had her bath," she added.

Brian's wash completed, he towelled himself dry and put on the pyjamas his mother had left for him in front of the fire.

"Tom," said Martha, "Tea will be ready in a minute."

"Alright, dear."

Brian and his father went into the kitchen and sat down at the table where Janey was placing the cutlery. Martha ladled the stew onto the plates and brought them over. Then she poured the water from the kettle into the teapot and set it down.

"Sorry everyone," Martha said. "We don't have much bread. There is still a shortage and we need to have some for tomorrow's breakfast. I had to queue for ages today to get the mutton."

"That's alright ma," said Janey. "This stew looks good and I'm so hungry, I could eat a horse!"

"You can't eat a horse," piped up Brian

"That would be cruel, wouldn't it da?"

"It's just an expression, son. Janey didn't mean it."

"Well, that's a silly thing to say," said Brian.

They all commenced eating except Tom who was pushing the food around his plate.

"Aren't you hungry dear?" asked Martha.

"No, don't seem to have much of an appetite."

"Well, have a cup of tea at least," she said as she poured the tea into his cup.

"Thanks," Tom said despondently.

"Are you still going to meet your mates tomorrow?"

"I'll see how I feel."

"It would be good for you to get out of the house and talk to other people. It's not good for you to be sitting around here moping all day."

Tom sat there looking down at his unfinished tea and started to shake. Martha got up and put her arm around his trembling shoulders. Janey and Brian looked at each other in dismay then hurriedly ate their food.

"Ma, can Brian and I leave the table?" asked Janey.

"Yes love, go and see if there is something on the wireless. I'll just get your father into bed and then you can help with the drying up."

Janey and Brian went into the sitting room and turned on the wireless while their mother escorted their father up to bed. They could hear him coughing as he went up the stairs. They settled down in front of the wireless and listened to one of their favourite serials.

"Janey," said Brian when there was a break in the broadcast.

"What?"

"Do you think da will get better?"

"I don't know Brian, I hope so. At least we have our da. Some of my friends at school don't have their fathers anymore. They were killed in the war."

"I don't like the war, or the Hun, Janey. Will there be another war?"

"No, Brian I don't think the government will let that happen. Anyway, not for a long time. Maybe when we aren't around anymore."

"Oh, that's good then," replied Brian who was picking his nose.

"Stop picking your nose, Brian, it's disgusting!"

Brian stopped the disgusting habit and resumed listening to the exploits of Buck Rogers as he rode off on another adventure.

***

"I say, Martha did you hear the latest?" asked Ethel, the local gossip from next door, church bazaar hair in curlers. They were pegging the washing and she was chomping at the bit to impart some news.

"Oh, hello Ethel. What did you hear?"

"Well, our Ernie heard that the barmaid at the Crown & Thistle was having it off with one of them yanks when Frank was away, and he caught them at it when he arrived home earlier than expected. She were always a brazen hussy that one! Wouldn't take her long to hook up with a Johnny when poor Frank was over there putting up with Gawd knows what!"

"Oh, really. Poor Frank. That's terrible Ethel."

"Yes, and that's not all. Frank took a swing at him and broke his jaw and now Frank is in the lock-up for assault."

"Oh, dear."

"Anyway, Martha, how's your Tom getting on? Haven't seen him around" she asked taking some more dolly pegs to hang up her commodious bloomers.

"He has good days and bad Ethel," answered Martha. "I am worried about him to tell you the truth. He has such terrible nightmares and can't seem to shake that cough. He was thinking about going to see some of his mates today but he is still in bed.

Last night he couldn't eat any tea. He hasn't much of an appetite."

"That's what the war does to them, Martha. I remember old Uncle Jack. He were affected bad by the mustard gas in the first war and he lost his leg. Terrible it was! And my Arthur, god rest his soul," she said blessing herself. "Shot to pieces in that hell at the Somme. I am sorry for you dearie. If you need anything just bang on the wall."

"Thanks very much, Ethel. Well, I'd better get on. I still have the towels to mangle and I must go and buy something for tonight's dinner. There was such a queue yesterday: I thought I would never be served."

"Yes, it's awful that queueing. Doesn't do me bunions any good and that's a fact! Give me regards to your Tom and tell him to keep his pecker up."

"Will do. See you later"

Martha went inside to rinse the towels and then went to check on Tom. Janey had gone to see a film with her friend, Maisie, and Brian was playing with his soldiers. Going into the kitchen she encountered Tom having a shave.

"Oh, there you are dear. Have you decided to go out?" she asked.

"Yes, love I think so."

"Well, that's splendid. Just give me a minute to tidy myself and I will come with you."

"You needn't bother. I will be alright."

"No, I have to go to the shop anyway, so it won't be any trouble. I will just put some lipstick on and grab my bag. Brian can come. A walk will do him good."

"Brian," Martha called. "I'm going up the street with your father and to the shop and I want you to come with me."

"Oh ma, do I have to? I haven't finished this game yet."

"Yes Brian, a walk will do you good. Get your coat like a good boy. I might buy you a chocolate."

"Alright, but can I have two chocolates?" he shouted.

"No, one is quite sufficient, now hurry up."

Rugged up against the cold, Tom and Martha, holding hands walked along the street with Brian trailing behind. They arrived at the pub where Tom was to meet his friends. Martha said goodbye and told him to enjoy himself and then seeing him safely inside went with Brian to the butchers to queue for some sausages. While standing there, she hoped that Tom would be alright and have a good time talking to his old mates. Brian was impatient to have his promised chocolate and kept whining about how long this was going to take and the lolly shop would be closed if they didn't hurry. Finally, they were served and Martha and Brian scurried to the shop to buy the long-awaited chocolate.

"Yum, that was good," said Brian, his mouth smeared with the remains of it.

"That's good, pet, glad you enjoyed it."

She took her handkerchief and spitting on it tried to wipe his mouth clean.

"Now, I want to pop into the pub to see how your father is getting on."

"Oh ma, do you have to. I want to go home and play with my soldiers."

"I won't be long Brian. I just bought you that chocolate so stop your whining."

On the brink of dyspeptic carousal, the pub was now heaving with people with a dart competition in full swing. Martha, with Brian in her wake, stepped inside and pushed her way through the crowd. She looked around trying to see Tom when her eyes alighted on one of his mates. Mike, who had been working in the same firm as Tom was also an accountant, and they had been together at the landing of Dunkirk. However, although seriously wounded resulting in the amputation of an arm, he had escaped back to Britain in one of the rescue boats and was ultimately invalided out of the army.

Tom had not been so fortunate, as before the flotilla arrived, he had been captured and force-marched for twenty days to the town of Trier, where he had been interred in a camp as a prisoner of the Germans.

From there, with many others, he had been put on a train and sent to work as a slave in the Siemens factory near Ravensbruck assembling parts for the German war planes. This work, which involved the inhalation of sulphur fumes as well as the terrible conditions in the camp, had all contributed to the poor condition of his lungs.

During the war, Mike's wife, June had been working at a place called Bletchley Park. She had said that it was a clerical position to do with the Department of Defence and required her to work long hours often during the night. Mike was not sure what it entailed as June was not keen to divulge much about it so he did not pester her.

Martha, pulling Brian along jostled her way through the crowd.

"Hello Mike," she said breathlessly. "Have you seen Tom? Only I left him here a little while ago. He was to meet up with you and some other fellows."

"Oh, hello Martha. Yes, he was here for a while. He said he was going back home. I tried to get him to stay and have a couple of pints but couldn't persuade him. He doesn't seem well."

"No, Mike he isn't."

"Is this your young fellow?" asked Mike pointing to Brian.

"Yes, this is Brian. Say hello to Mr. Williams, Brian. He is a friend of your father."

"Hello," said Brian.

"Pleased to meet you, young man," said Mike extending his hand but Brian pulled away.

"Mike, I had better be going and make sure Tom is safe at home," said Martha anxiously.

"Yes, you do that. I'm sure he got there safely. I will come and visit him soon if that's alright with you. Poor Tom, I hate to see him like this. If there is anything I can do to help Martha, just say the word."

"Thanks, Mike. That's awfully good of you, and come over whenever you like. I'm sure Tom would appreciate it. He spends most of the time inside."

"Right you are," said Mike. "Is Tuesday convenient?"

"Yes, that will be fine."

"Well, tell the old boy I will see him then, and I will be carrying a bottle of stout. That should cheer him up. I don't know if June can come. She seems to still be occupied at night with work commitments. Anyway, probably it would be better if I came on my own this time."

"Yes, maybe that would be a better plan. You can always bring her when Tom has improved. Come for tea around six thirty. It won't be anything fancy, just the usual rationed fare I'm afraid."

"Brian, say goodbye to Mr. Williams. He is coming to have tea with us next week."

"Bye, Mr. Williams" muttered Brian.

"Goodbye young man, and goodbye Martha. See you all on Tuesday."

"Ma," said Brian as they walked out of the pub.

"Yes, pet."

"Why does Mr. Williams only have one arm?"

"He lost it in the war, Brian."

"Oh, but couldn't they find it and sew it on?"

"No pet, it was too badly damaged for that. Now let's get a move on. It's feeling a bit chilly, and I want to see how your father is."

They hurried home to Tom who they found snoring in his chair. Quickly a blanket was procured from the bedroom and Martha covered her sleeping husband. She then set a match to the kindling and before long there was a fire warming the room. Then she took the washing off the line, hung it on the rack above the stove, mangled the towels and put them on the line, then went to see about preparing the sausages for tea. Brian had scuttled off to finish his game and Janey was expected to return from her outing very soon.

Chapter Two

"Are you coming to church Tom?" asked Martha as she was putting on her gown.

It was Sunday and, as the fog swirled around outside the window, she pulled the gown tighter around her.

"Don't think I am up to it dear," replied Tom. "I didn't seem to get much sleep last night."

"No, you didn't. Never mind, you stay there and keep warm and I'll bring you up a nice cup of tea and a slice of toast and marmalade."

"Thanks, darling," he said. "Sorry I'm such a burden lately" as another paroxysm of coughing overtook him.

"That's alright. There are better times ahead. Ethel next door said to keep your pecker up."

"Oh, Ethel. Is she still the local gossip?"

"Yes, she is. As a matter of fact, she told me yesterday the barmaid at the pub was sleeping with one of the Americans while her husband was away. He arrived home unexpectedly early and caught them in the act. He broke the fellow's jaw and now he's in jail."

"Oh, well I don't think he will be the only one in that situation. Those Americans are pretty brash, luring our womenfolk with their money and charms."

"Yes, they seem to have a reputation. I've heard that they are overpaid, oversexed, and over here," she said brightly. "Well, better get moving. Have to get the children up and fed. I don't like being late for church. The vicar takes a dim view of late comers and makes you feel frightfully embarrassed. Oh, Tom, are we still going to lunch at your mother's today?"

"I suppose so. She will be expecting us."

"But surely she will understand if we don't go especially when she knows you are not that well."

"I should be alright if I just have a rest while you are all at church."

"You know best Tom, but I think she should make allowances. We can't go over every Sunday."

"Yes dear, now you run along before you're late."

Martha kissed Tom on the forehead and then went over to the dresser to pour the water into the bowl to wash her face. As she washed, she thought about Tom's mother whom she did not like very much. She was a widow and lived in Belgravia, her late husband having made his fortune in the railways, although she herself was quite parsimonious. Her haughty demeanour made Martha quite intimidated, and Tom's childhood had been tainted by her aloofness towards him. She thought that Tom could have done much better for himself than being a lowly accountant in a shipping office, and Martha had the impression that her marriage had also disappointed her, as she would have liked her son with someone a bit more uppity than she. Also, she had not wanted Tom to go to war and did not hesitate to mention it whenever they visited. All in all, it was not conducive for pleasant Sunday outings.

She hurried to wake the children, but they were already in the kitchen where Janey was buttering a slice of toast for Brian.

"Hello, my darlings. Did you have a good sleep?"

"Yes, ma," replied Janey. "I had such a lovely dream."

"Did you?" asked Martha. "About what?"

"It was about the picture I saw yesterday, Alice in Wonderland. I dreamt it was me at the mad hatter's tea party and I was dancing with the dormouse and the white rabbit. It felt so real ma," said Janey. "Then, just as I was enjoying myself, I woke up."

"It is annoying when you are enjoying a dream and then awaken not to know how it was going to end," said Martha filling the kettle.

"I didn't have a dream," said Brian as he licked the jam off the knife.

"Brian don't put the knife in your mouth," cried Janey.

"No, Brian, that's naughty, you know not to do that," added Martha.

Martha made the tea and grilled a slice of toast for her and Tom.

"Have you finished your breakfast?" she asked Janey and Brian.

"Yes, ma," chorused the children.

"Then clean your teeth and get dressed. I won't be long. I just have to take this up to your father. We don't want to be late again for church."

"Come on Brian," said Janey. "I'll help you do up your laces. You take forever when you do them."

"Can I wear my red jumper? I like that one the best."

"Alright, but only if it's clean. You can't wear dirty clothes to church."

They trooped off to the bedroom leaving Martha to finish her breakfast. Sipping the last drop of tea, she set about putting Tom's on the tray. As she took it up to him she hoped he would have an appetite and be able to eat it.

"Tom," she whispered. "Are you awake?"

"Oh, hello dear. I must have dropped off," he said hauling himself up from the bed.

"Here's some breakfast," said Martha putting the tray on his lap.

"Thanks. How are the children? Are they going to church with you?"

"Yes, Tom they are, and hopefully they're getting themselves ready."

Martha went to the wardrobe to look for something to wear. She selected her brown skirt and yellow twinset and also her brown overcoat. Her brown brogues were on the floor beside the chair where she had left them yesterday. She went to the mirror and brushed her hair then put on her hat. Then she powdered her face and applied some lipstick.

"All ready?" asked Tom "You look nice."

"Oh, these old things," replied Martha. "Now try and have some more sleep and I will see you shortly. Do you need anything else before I go?"

"No, I don't think so love, thanks."

Martha straightened the eiderdown and kissing her husband went to fetch Janey and Brian who were in the lounge room listening to the wireless.

"Right, let's go," said Martha as she took her bag from the hallstand.

As they left the house the wind had sprung up blowing the leaves around their feet. The fog had lifted and there was a weak sun doing its best to appear more brightly.

"Just as well we have our coats," Martha said to the children. "It's not very warm out."

"Ma," said Brian.

"Yes, pet."

"Are we going to grandma's today?"

"Probably, Brian, we'll see how your father is when we come back from church."

"I don't like going to grandma's."

"Why?"

"Well, she doesn't ever give me big hugs like nanna and she always tells me to mind my manners."

"Oh, pet that is just her way. Everyone is different. She is your father's mother and so we should try to get along with her when we visit. It's only on Sundays after all, not every day."

Brian kicked a stone along the footpath not feeling very cheerful. Up ahead, Janey was walking along humming a tune from the film she saw last night. At least one of them is happy thought, Martha.

They arrived at the church, and finding a pew, clambered in, Brian managing to step on an aged lady's foot who gave them all a disdainful look. Martha whispering an apology, sat down and commenced opening the hymn book. Everyone stood as the vicar walked up to the pulpit and announced the first hymn which was Every Morning Mercies New. Martha and Janey joined in the refrain of the other parishioners while Brian looked around to see if he could spot any of his friends amongst the throng.

During the sermon which turned out to be quite a long one, the vicar extolling everyone to heed the word of God and not give into temptation, Brian commenced fidgeting which resulted in Martha giving him a nudge and a contemptuous look. Then, kneeling, she prayed that God would make her husband better and give her the strength to carry on looking after her family.

The service over, Martha and the children walked out of the church to be met at the door by the vicar.

"Good morning, Martha," he said. "And good morning children."

"Good morning vicar," replied Martha. "Janey and Brian, say good morning to the vicar."

"Hello, vicar," they both replied.

"And how is poor Tom?" he asked.

"Not very well, I'm afraid vicar."

"Sorry to hear that my dear. The war has taken a terrible toll. I will say a prayer for him."

"Thank you," said Martha with tears threatening to fall from her eyes.

Patting her arm, the vicar added.

"Try not to worry too much, these things are sent to try us, and we just have to offer our suffering up to him."

Taking a handkerchief from her bag to wipe her eyes, Martha nodded and then gathering up the children commenced walking home.

"Don't cry ma," Janey said as she noticed her mother's sadness.

"Oh, I'm alright darling."

"Why are you crying?" asked Brian pulling on Martha's coat.

"Ma's just a bit sad today that's all pet. Everyone feels sad sometimes, don't they?"

"I felt sad when Tilly died."

"Yes, you did, but at least she is in a better place now and not in any more pain, is she?"

"Is she in heaven?"

"Yes pet, she is in cat heaven."

Arriving at the house Martha unlocked the door and they all trooped inside. Tom was up and dressed and sitting in his chair. Martha went straight over and put her arms around him.

Janey took off her coat and helped her brother out of his then Brian scrambled over to his father.

"Da, are we going to grandma's today?" he asked.

"Yes son, I believe we are."

"Are you sure you are up to it dear?" Martha asked.

"Yes, I will be alright. I dozed a bit when you were at church. Did you talk to anyone we know?"

"No, not really, only the vicar."

"Suppose he gave you the usual platitudes, saying he will pray for me and so on."

"He tries to be helpful Tom."

"Well, I don't need his help or God's either. There wasn't much of it around when I was in the camp, I can tell you," Tom said getting breathless.

"Now, don't get yourself upset. I will put the kettle on and we will have a nice cup of tea before we leave. There might be some music to listen to."

Going over, she switched on the wireless, and through the airwaves came the voices of the Andrews sisters. Martha went to the kitchen to boil the kettle and Brian raced upstairs to play with his train. Janey settled down on the floor to read her book beside her father who was still coughing occasionally.

A knock at the door.

Martha thought who could it be on Sunday morning? Putting the tea cosy on the pot she went to the door and found it was Ethel.

"Oh, hello Ethel," she said.

"Hello, dearie. Just thought you might like these," she said as she thrust a plate of biscuits at her.

"Oh, thank you Ethel. I've just made a pot of tea. Would you like to come in and have a cup with us?"

"Don't mind if I do," replied Ethel stepping inside.

"Tom," called Martha. "Ethel's here and she brought us some biscuits."

"Hello Tom," Ethel said as she walked into the room. "How're you going?"

"Not bad Ethel," Tom replied despondently.

Janey looked up and said hello and then resumed reading.

"The tea's ready everyone," Martha called out.

"Janey, can you run upstairs and see if Brian wants to come down and have a biscuit and some milk, please?"

"Alright, ma," said Janey and as she got up off the floor her father left his chair and went into the kitchen where the two women were already seated.

"As I was telling you, Martha," Ethel said as she started dunking her biscuit in the tea. "That floosy from the pub looks in the family way to me. As I was saying to Aggie Mason," but she did not finish the conversation as just then Janey came in with Brian, and Martha put her finger to her lips to silence Ethel's talk. Brian sat down and, grabbing a biscuit wasted no time stuffing it into his mouth.

"Go easy, son," admonished his father.

"Yes, Brian don't eat it all at once. We don't want you choking for goodness sake," said his mother.

"Do you want a biscuit, Tom?"

"No thanks, I'll pass. I'll save my appetite for dinner."

"Are you going out for your dinner then?" asked Ethel helping herself to another biscuit.

"Yes, we are going to Tom's mother. We usually go every Sunday. It is something of a ritual."

"What time train are you catching?" asked Ethel.

"Probably the 11:30," said Tom looking at his watch.

"Well, mustn't keep you then. Them trains don't run too much to schedule these days, especially on Sundays," said Ethel as she pushed back the chair and started walking to the door.

"Ta ra, enjoy yourselves," she yelled.

Martha saw her out and thanking her for the biscuits set about clearing up the kitchen. She could hear Tom coughing as he made his way upstairs to tell the children they all had to leave soon if they were to catch the next train.

"Tom," Martha said as they were en route to Belgravia.

"Yes, darling."

"Did I tell you that Mike is coming over on Tuesday for tea?"

"No, you didn't."

"It was when I was looking for you in the pub. We started talking and he said he would like to see you so I suggested that he could come on Tuesday."

"Is he coming on his own?"

"Yes, apparently June seems to be occupied most nights, so she won't be coming?"

"Well, I suppose that will be alright."

"That's good, dear. Mike is a good friend. The pair of you can have a chin wag," said Martha patting his hand.

Tom stared blankly out the window, his mind in a place filled with the spectres of sick starving men and burly Germans in jackboots. He rubbed his forehead and pulled a handkerchief from his pocket as another coughing episode overtook him.

They arrived at Grandma Johnson's after walking for 15 minutes from the station. Tom's feet, still suffering from the blisters he had sustained, and the condition of his lungs all made for a slow journey. Eventually, they arrived, and, after ringing the bell once, the door was opened by a tall lugubrious-looking woman clad in black, hair pulled tightly back into a bun, doing nothing to enhance her sharp features.

"Oh, here you are at last," she said superciliously looking down at the visitors.

"Yes, here we are," said Tom.

"Well, come in then, and you children, don't forget to take off your shoes. The floors were polished yesterday, and I don't want any dirt brought in."

Janey and Brian unlaced their shoes and placed them at the door. Tom and Martha did the same and then followed the hostess through the foyer, the floor gleaming with black and white tiles. Leading the way into the sitting room they were told to sit. Tom and Martha sat on the chesterfield under a painting by Turner while the children perched on the two easy chairs. As grandma's maid Phyllis offered Tom and Martha glasses of sherry and the children lemonade, the painting on the wall drew Janey's interest as was always the case whenever she visited her grandma.

"Now," said grandma. "How are you all and especially you Thomas? I hope you have got rid of that nasty cough of yours."

"No, mother as a matter of fact I haven't. I can't seem to shake it."

"Well, Martha," she said looking over at her. "Don't you think it's about time you took your husband to the doctor to see about it?"

"It's not Martha's fault mother," Tom responded. "I don't think there is much the doctors can do. It's just a matter of waiting for it to settle down."

"Settle down!" she railed. "I don't think that is going to happen. I blame that war Thomas, for everything that's happened to you. If you had been sensible and listened to me and not gone running off to fight you would not be feeling like this!"

"Now, mother we have been over this many times. Can't you just drop it?"

Grandma sniffed and took a big swig of her sherry.

Brian then piped up.

"Grandma, when are we having our dinner, I'm hungry!"

"Well!" spluttered grandma. "We will be dining when I say. And, for your information, it is called luncheon, not dinner. It's about time you learnt some manners, young man. As far as I'm concerned, little boys should be seen and not heard!"

Martha went over to comfort her son who had now started crying and Janey whispered that she was going to the lavatory which was of course inside the house and not outside as theirs was.

Grandma called after her to make sure she pulled the chain when she had finished and also to wash her hands thoroughly with the soap. Janey, sitting on the lavatory pondered over the strained relationship of her grandma with their family. She, like her brother, wished that grandma was more like their mother's mother who was always cheerful and friendly, and a visit to her was something to look forward to and not dread. However, their nanna lived in Cornwall so school holidays were when they could spend some time with her. It was so exciting packing their suitcases and taking the train to the seaside, knowing that at the end of their journey they would be in the big embrace of their beloved nanna.

Perched atop a craggy cliff, her cottage exuded such a sense of warmth and peace it was almost tangible, especially when the children tucked up in their beds heard the waves whipped up by a nightly storm crashing onto the rocks below.

In the mornings, fresh eggs were gathered from the hen house and there was always a competition to see which child could collect the most eggs. Brian, being the youngest, tended to break a few in his haste to claim victory! Lucy the goat and Harold the pig made up the rest of nanna's menagerie.

Granddad's Scottish father had built ships at Clydeside in Glasgow, and granddad, employed by the West Cornwall Steamship Co had piloted a steamship called The Lyonesse which had sailed from Cornwall to the Scilly Isles. Sometimes, nanna was able to accompany him on these voyages and, as she had an artistic flair, this resulted in many sketches of the beautiful wildflowers which nestled in the Isles' many coves.

When the great war was declared, he enlisted with the Royal Navy but was to die in the great battle of Jutland when his ship HMS Tipperary was sunk with all hands by a German warship.

Martha grew up not knowing her father, but her mother's abundant love more than made up for his absence. Many days saw her with her easel painting scenes of the Cornish coastline while her daughter frolicked in the waves.

"Janey," she heard her mother call at the door.

"Are you finished, darling? Only grandma has our dinner ready."

"Coming," Janey replied, and pulling the chain she pulled up her knickers and then made sure she washed her hands with the perfumed soap as instructed.

Martha and her daughter walked downstairs to the dining room where Tom, Brian, and grandma were already seated. On the table covered by a white linen cloth was a cold collation of meat and salad with condiments in silver cruets. A crystal pitcher of water and glasses completed the scene.

"Now," said grandma. "At last we are all here. Thomas, please say grace."

The assembled group bowed their heads as Tom gave thanks for the meal that his mother had provided. In silence, they helped themselves to the food as grandma ensured that no one was having more than their share. Martha poured the water into their glasses, and they all commenced eating.

"How is your sciatica, Sylvia?" asked Martha breaking the silence, as she spooned some mustard on her meat. "Any better?"

"No, I'm still suffering. The damp weather does not help," she replied.

"Brian don't put your elbows on the table!" she added admonishing Brian.

"It's the height of rudeness. When are you going to learn how to behave in society?"

"Sorry, grandma" mumbled Brian.

As he reached for the sauce, he managed to knock over his glass sending a stream of water all over the tablecloth.

"Oh, no, if that isn't the last straw you clumsy boy! Can't you do anything right? Can't you ask for someone to pass the sauce? You're just like your father was forever knocking things over!" she railed.

"Now, mother, it's only water," said Tom commencing to blot it up with his napkin.

Martha went around to Brian who had turned red with the shame of it all and was threatening to cry again. Janey put her arm around her little brother and whispered something in his ear which seemed to cheer him a little.

"Sorry, Sylvia," said Martha. "Accidents will happen with children."

"Not all children, Martha," she responded dabbing her mouth "At least Janey shows some decorum."

"I think we should have our tea in the kitchen where there will be less to damage," she added rising from the table with a swish of her skirt.

Martha whispered to Tom that she did not want to stay much longer, and Tom agreed saying they could be on the two-thirty train if they drank their tea quickly. Finally, with no more mishaps, they bade goodbye to grandma. After managing to catch the train with only a few minutes to spare Martha, Tom and their family were on their way to the comfort of their own home at Ealing with Martha declaring to Tom her intention to decline any more invitations to luncheons.

Chapter Three

"Brian, hurry up, you'll be late for school," cried Martha.

"But ma, I can't find my pencil case," replied Brian.

It was the usual Monday morning mayhem and Martha was running around making breakfast, the lunches for school and now trying to find the errant pencil case.

"Did you bring it home on Friday?" asked Martha.

"Yes, I think so, but maybe I didn't," said Brian as he commenced pulling the bedroom apart.

"Well, you can't look for it all day. It's probably still in your desk. Come on, you'll make Janey late as well if you don't get a move on."

"But ma, if it's not there what will I write with?"

"Just tell Miss Stubbs and she will give you a pencil. I will look for it today. It's bound to be somewhere around the place."

Janey was waiting at the door for her brother.

"Come on Brian. Why don't you make sure you have everything before we have to leave for school?"

Martha helped Brian with his satchel and ensuring his mouth looked clean saw the children to the door.

"Bye ma," they said.

"Bye pets, have a good day," replied Martha.

She went upstairs to check on Tom whose sleep was still being interrupted by nightmares and coughing and this morning she had noticed spots of blood on his pillowcase. This, combined with her mother-in-law's suggestion, made Martha more concerned. She made up her mind to tell Tom they would see a doctor today for another check-up.

"Morning, dear," said Martha as she kissed him.

"Hello, darling. Children gone to school?"

"Yes, at last. Brian couldn't find his pencil case and spent half the morning looking for it."

"Nothing changes," replied Tom.

"No, I'm afraid it doesn't."

"Tom."

"Yes, dear."

"I was thinking maybe you should see another doctor. Get a second opinion about that cough."

"Did mother have anything to do with it?"

"Not really, but I suppose she reinforced what I have been concerned about and also I noticed there were spots of blood on your pillow this morning."

"Oh, are there? I must have had a nosebleed during the night, but we'll go if you are concerned."

"Well, it can't hurt. You won't have much to lose by seeing someone and might have everything to gain."

"That's true, I suppose," Tom said running his hand through his hair.

He got up and went to wash his face and Martha put his trousers, shirt, and jumper on the bed. His shoes were where he left them last night by the dresser.

"Your clothes are all ready for you Tom. I'll make you some breakfast. Do you feel like some powdered egg?"

"Yes, thanks darling, but only a little," said Tom as he commenced stepping into his trousers.

On the way to the kitchen, Martha saw that the paper and mail had been delivered and, picking it up, noticed there was a flyer about the upcoming street party next Saturday. She hoped Tom would be well enough to attend with her and the children as it would be an opportunity for them to socialise with their neighbours.

Putting the mail on the table to read later, she commenced preparing her husband's breakfast. Being Monday, there was the wash to be dealt with and the sheets to be changed, but it was more important that she take Tom to the doctor.

As she put on the kettle the telephone rang.

"Hello," answered Martha.

"Hello, Martha," said her best friend Helen. "How are you?"

"Oh, Helen, nice of you to ring. I'm just making some breakfast for Tom."

"How is he?" asked Helen.

"Not so good. I'm so worried about him Helen. He is still coughing and doesn't sleep very well, and this morning I noticed spots of blood on his pillowcase. As a matter of fact, I am taking him to the doctor today to get another opinion."

"Oh no, sorry to hear that. What did the other medico say?"

"He seemed to think it wasn't serious and would settle down in time, but it's been going on too long."

"Well, I think you are doing the right thing. He might need an x-ray. God knows what he may have picked up in that camp or that other place of horrors!"

"Yes, that's what I have been thinking. I hope it's not serious," said Martha.

"Fingers crossed. How are the children?"

"They're well thank goodness, and how is your mum?"

Helen's mother had been bedridden for some time and recently had suffered a stroke, so Helen had resigned from the hospital where she had been a nurse, to care for her. The two friends had met at the boarding house and as Helen's flatmate was vacating, and Martha was looking for accommodation, they had decided to share.

Helen had been Martha's bridesmaid which had thrilled her as it was always her wish to fall in love but as her time was spent caring for her mother, there was not much time for her to meet anyone suitable.

"Oh, she has good days and bad but lately the bad seem to be more numerous I'm afraid," replied Helen.

"Oh, so sorry to hear that, Helen. Give her my love. I will try to pop around to see you both. How does Saturday sound? There is the street party on but I could come over after that. I really don't want to stay there all day."

"Alright, Saturday sounds perfect. She would love to see you, Martha. By the way, did you go on your Sunday sojourn to the curmudgeon's?"

"Yes, we did. It was a nightmare as usual. Brian put his foot in it and to make matters worse, ended up spilling water over the linen tablecloth!"

"Blimey, I'll bet that set her off."

"Yes, she is certainly a difficult woman. I wish Tom would stand up to her. But she has always ruled with an iron fist. Even her husband was dominated from what I've heard. Tom said he used to make himself scarce. If he wasn't locked in his study he would be away at meetings and so on."

"Poor fellow, having a mother like that. Well, I'd better let you go. Love to Tom and the children and good luck at the doctors."

"Thanks, Helen. See you soon and love to Val," said Martha.

She put the telephone down and raced into the kitchen.

"Was that Helen?" asked Tom as he came in.

"Yes, it was," said Martha beating the egg mixture and putting it on the stove.

"How is she and how is her mother?"

"She said she seems well and has good days and bad. The poor woman has had that infirmity for so long and now to be suffering from a stroke," said Martha as she spooned their egg onto the plates.

"Yes, it's a wonder she is still alive. It would be awful being bedridden like that. I would hate it," said Tom as he started eating.

Pouring their tea, she told him she would try to pop around to see them soon.

Breakfast finished, Tom took the paper and went into the lounge room to read while Martha cleared the detritus from the table and started washing up. She thought about all the chores she had to do, one of which was to buy something for tonight's tea and for tomorrow when Mike was due to come. Maybe we can have fish tonight if the fishmonger has any available and tomorrow, I can make a cottage pie. She pulled the plug and let the dirty water flow down the drain and then taking the tea towel started to dry the plates. As she dried, she remembered to look for Brian's pencil case.

She went upstairs and into Brian's room which was in a state of upheaval as books and clothes had been strewn around in her son's efforts to locate the missing case. Putting everything away in its rightful place Martha then stripped the sheets off the bed and as she did her foot connected with something hard. Looking underneath the bed, her eyes alighted on the lost pencil case. Thank goodness, she thought, that is one less thing to worry about. She collected the sheets from the other beds and took them downstairs to the copper with the intention of washing them tomorrow then, after making the beds with fresh sheets, went to tidy herself for the trip to the doctor.

"Mr. Johnson," said the rosy-cheeked receptionist. "Please take a seat, I'm afraid you will have to wait. There are five patients already ahead of you."

Martha and Tom sat down in a room full of people all waiting to have their illnesses diagnosed. There were two obviously pregnant women who were both busy knitting bootees for their expectant babies, a young man whose arm was heavily bandaged, and a little boy who was being continually admonished by his frazzled mother as he kept wiping his runny nose with the back of his hand and then wiping it on his trousers.

Martha took a magazine from the table and leafed through it but found she could not concentrate as she kept envisaging the worst-case scenario for her husband. She prayed that this doctor would have some answers and be able to make him well again. Tom sat looking at the floor, his feet moving about nervously. Martha patted his hand and forced herself to smile.

"How are you feeling dear?" she asked.

"Not too bad. But I wish we didn't have to wait," replied Tom.

"I know, but it can't be helped. Do you want to read something?"

"No, I'm right."

After what seemed an eternity, the doctor, at last, called them in.

"Take a seat please," said the doctor.

"Well, Tom, is it? Pleased to meet you. And this is your wife?"

"Yes, doctor this is Martha."

"Hello," said the doctor.

"Hello, doctor."

"Now, what brings you here today?" the doctor asked.

"Well, doctor," said Tom. "I have this cough which doesn't seem to be improving."

"Ah, yes," said the doctor. "Your records here say you have spent some time as a prisoner of war."

"Yes, doctor, that is correct."

"And it also says," said the doctor surveying the notes on his desk, "that you were involved with assembling parts for aircraft."

"That's right doctor. The conditions were not very good. There were sulphur fumes, and we didn't have access to any masks."

"I see," said the doctor stroking his beard.

"Well Tom, let's have a listen to your chest, shall we?"

"Just unbutton your shirt if you wouldn't mind."

Martha helped Tom with his shirt and then the doctor put the stethoscope on Tom's back and chest and told him to breathe deeply.

Then he looked down Tom's throat and felt his glands at the sides of his neck.

"Do you have any other symptoms?" asked the doctor.

"There was blood on his pillow this morning, doctor," Martha interjected.

"I see. Tom, have you noticed any blood when you cough lately?"

"Just a little, doctor," replied Tom looking sheepish.

"Oh, Tom," cried Martha. "Why didn't you tell me?"

"It hasn't been much, dear. I didn't want you to worry."

The doctor commenced writing some notes on the file and then sat back in his chair fingers intertwined.

"Tom, I am sending you straight to the hospital to have an x-ray."

"Oh doctor, what do you think he has?" asked Martha feeling terrified.

"Well, we will know more after he has the x-ray, but in my opinion, I think it may be TB."

"TB? Oh no!" cried Martha starting to cry.

"There, darling," said Tom trying to comfort her. "Don't get upset. We don't know anything yet. It may be a false alarm."

"Yes," said the doctor. "we will hope that it is. But go now to the hospital. Here is your referral."

"Excuse me doctor," interjected Martha. "Tom is still having these terrible nightmares. Is there anything that can be done for that?"

"I would say that they should become less as time goes on," replied the doctor. "But, in the meantime," he added opening a drawer and fossicking around. "Here are some sedatives to tide him over."

"Oh, thank you, doctor," Martha said as she took the bottle and the referral.

"Yes, thank you," added Tom.

Martha took Tom's hand, and they made their way to Ealing Hospital where their fate awaited them one way or the other.

Although the hospital was on Uxbridge Road, they decided to take a bus as they had already walked to the doctor's surgery and Martha knew Tom was in no condition to walk much further.

Arriving at the emergency entrance, Martha asked an orderly where the x-ray department was. He told them to go down the corridor, turn right near the lift, and there they would see the sign. Thanking him they followed his directions and soon were sitting waiting to be called.

"Tom," said Martha.

"Yes, dear."

"Do you still want Mike to come tomorrow for tea?"

"Yes, if it is no bother for you. Do you think he oughtn't to come?"

"No, I just thought with all that is happening you might not want to see him."

"I think I can handle old Mike."

"That's good then. He might cheer us up."

Just then the radiologist called them in. Tom was asked to put on a gown and then, standing in front of the machine was told to breathe in and hold his breath while the radiologist took the x-ray. Outwardly Martha was trying to remain calm for her husband's sake but inwardly she was a nervous wreck. The x-ray was completed; they were asked to wait for the results which had then to be taken back to the doctors.

"Well, that wasn't so bad was it?" Tom said to Martha who was holding on to the fateful package as they were seated again on the bus.

"No, I suppose not. I wonder when the doctor will tell us the result?"

"I don't want to wait for it now. I will ask the receptionist if they can ring us," said Tom.

"Yes, that would be best, dear. The time is getting on and the children will be home from school soon and I still have the fish to buy."

Arriving at the surgery, Tom handed over the x-ray and after being told that the doctor would ring them as soon as he could, Tom walked slowly home as Martha ducked into the fish mongers in an attempt to buy their tea.

The sheets were boiling in the copper and Martha was writing a shopping list when she heard the telephone ringing.

"I'll get it dear" announced Tom as he put down the paper and walked to the hall.

"Hello," he said.

"Hello. May I speak to Mr. Johnson please?" asked the caller.

"Yes, speaking" replied Tom.

"Oh, hello Tom, it's doctor Burns here."

"Hello, doctor."

"Tom, I have seen your x-ray and read the report and I'm afraid the news is not good."

"Oh," said Tom twisting the cord around his finger.

"Yes, sorry to tell you this but you do have TB. However, it is in the early stages and with appropriate rest and treatment you may have a full recovery."

"I see," said Tom as he spotted Martha appearing from the kitchen with an anxious look on her face. "Do you think it was because of the sulphur, doctor?"

"No, I don't think it was necessarily, although it would not have helped. The most probable cause was when you were in the camp. I have heard it was pretty rife in those places."

"What will the treatment be then?" asked Tom.

"The favoured treatment at present is a stay in a sanitarium. I can book you into Brompton which is 5 guineas a week all-inclusive or there is a private room available at Frimley which is slightly cheaper at 4 guineas."

"Oh, where are these places doctor?" asked Tom.

"They are in Surrey, about 130 miles southwest of London."

"And how long would I be staying there?"

"Well, as your right lung is affected and the x-ray showed a cavity, you would probably be looking at 6-9 months."

"That long?" cried Tom.

"Yes, I'm afraid so. That is about the average time give or take a few months. The main thing is to get you better."

"Yes, if that is what it takes then I will have to put up with it."

"Good man, that's the spirit. Well, have a chat with your wife and when you are ready let me know what you decide. But I cannot stress enough, do not be too long thinking about it. Time is of the essence!"

"Yes, thank you, doctor. We will let you know as soon as possible and thank you for ringing."

"Very well, goodbye Tom, and make sure you have plenty of rest in the meantime. Do not exert yourself in any way."

"No, I won't. Goodbye doctor."

"Goodbye, Tom."

Tom put down the telephone and taking Martha by the hand they went into the lounge room where he told her everything the doctor had said. Bursting into tears, she put her arms around her husband and thought her heart would break. Then, drying her eyes with the apron asked Tom how on earth were they going to afford the cost of the hospital.

"I will ask mother for a loan," he said.

"Your mother?" she cried. "She would never countenance anything like that."

"Well, it's worth a try. Surely if she knows it's my life that's at stake."

"I don't think much of your chances, dear but I suppose you can sound her out."

"Yes, as a matter of fact, I will ring her this minute before I lose my courage. Strike while the iron is hot" he said trying to put on a brave face.

"Very well then, dear. You do what you think is best. I had better get off to the shops before they run out of everything. I still have the sheets to finish."

"Alright, darling, sorry I can't help you with everything. Thank you for looking after us the way you do."

"Oh, fiddle-faddle. Just doing my job," said Martha playfully ruffling his hair. "Now after you talk to your mother take it easy as the doctor suggested."

"All I seem to do is take it easy. I'll be glad to go back to work."

"Well, after your treatment and you are cured you can look forward to that. I'm sure the office will be only too pleased to have you back. A good worker like you."

Martha left the house for the shops leaving Tom to deal with his mother. It would be a miracle if she loaned them the money being the skinflint that she was. She wished they had more money. It was all such a worry.

The queues at the shops were as bad as ever, but eventually, Martha had bought all the things on her list. She was just going in the gate when Ethel yelled out,

"Oi, Martha how's things ducks? Tom any better?"

"Oh, hello Ethel. Tom saw the doctor yesterday and had a chest x-ray. We're waiting for the results."

"Oh, x-ray you say? That doesn't sound good. Old Bruce from 46 had one of them and they found out it was cancer."

"Oh, that's awful. Sorry, Ethel, I can't stop and chat. Tom's friend, Mike is coming for tea, and I must get on with the preparations."

"Alright love, won't keep you, see you later," said Ethel stamping out her cigarette and going inside.

Martha struggled through to the kitchen with her basket full of groceries.

"I just bumped into Ethel," Martha said to Tom who was at the table drinking a cup of tea.

"She asked how you were. I didn't tell her we had the result of the x-ray. I really didn't feel up to it."

"No, don't blame you. We haven't even told the children," replied Tom.

"Did you manage to ring your mother while I was out?"

"Yes, I did."

"I don't suppose she is going to loan us the money?"

"No. It was as I expected. She railed and ranted about my going to the war and bringing everything on myself. She really is heartless."

"She certainly is, and with all the money she has. It's not as if she can't afford it. She really takes the cake, Tom. I couldn't care if we never see her again," Martha said, eyes blazing with fury.

Tom stared at the table looking disheartened and Martha went over and put her arms around him said.

"I will ring my mother tomorrow. Maybe she might be able to help us. I have to tell her your prognosis anyway."

"Alright, but don't put any pressure on her."

"No, Tom I won't, and if she can't manage anything I'm sure something will turn up," said Martha.

"We have to tell the children when they come home," Tom said as another coughing attack overwhelmed him.

Martha as she took the large pan from the cupboard in readiness for the cottage pie.

"We had better tell them before Mike comes over," suggested Tom.

"Yes, oh Tom, I hope they don't get too upset," she said as she commenced chopping some carrots and potatoes.

"Janey should take it in her stride. She's a mature 12-year-old but as for Brian, that might be a different story," said Tom.

They heard the front door open and then in marched the children.

"Hello, poppets. Did you have a good day at school?" asked Martha.

"Not bad, ma," replied Janey putting her satchel in the corner.

"And how was your day, Brian?" asked Tom.

"I fell over and hurt my knee," said Brian dumping his satchel on the floor and showing his father the skinned knee.

"That's not good old chap. We had better put some iodine on it so it won't get infected."

"Iodine stings!" cried Brian.

"It only stings for a minute though," said his father.

"Guess what Brian?" said Martha.

"What?"

"I found your pencil case!"

Brian's face lit up and he momentarily forgot about his sore knee.

"Where was it ma?"

"It was under your bed, chicken."

"Is it in my room now?"

"Yes, it is, and make sure you don't lose it again. Did Miss Stubbs give you a pencil to write with?"

"Yes. Ma, I'm hungry. Can I have something to eat?"

"Yes, pet. Just give me a minute to brown the mince and I will get you and Janey a biscuit. You know Mr. Williams is coming for tea tonight so don't eat too much. Now go with your da and see to that knee in the meantime."

"Alright."

Tom took his son over to the medicine cupboard and taking a wad of cotton wool and the bottle of iodine started to dab his knee.

"Ow, that hurts da," cried Brian.

"Sorry sport," said Tom.

He put the iodine away, and then Brian, grabbing two biscuits from the plate bolted upstairs to fetch his pencil case.

Martha added the beef stock and set the meat to simmer then she called Brian to come down as she and his father had something to tell him and his sister.

"Can we visit you there da?" asked Janey after they had been told the news.

"Yes, pet," said Martha "I will take you and Brian on the train on weekends."

"Why can't da stay here with us?" asked Brian.

"Because da has a serious disease, darling and he must stay in a special hospital where he will be looked after properly," answered Martha.

"That's right. And you will be the man of the house while I'm away and take care of your ma and your sister," said Tom coughing into his handkerchief and then hurriedly stuffing it into his pocket lest the children see any blood.

Brian thought for a bit then said if he was going to be the man around here he was going to stay up late and listen to the wireless. That thought was quickly knocked on the head though to Brian's dismay, and he went back up to his room to play with his train until it was time for dinner.

Mike arrived punctually at six thirty armed with his promised bottle of stout.

"I say, Martha," said Mike as he sniffed the air. "Something smells good."

"It's only cottage pie, I'm afraid Mike," replied Martha. She thanked him for the proffered bottle as she placed it on the table.

"Go into the lounge room. Tom is in there. I will join you in a minute."

As Mike entered the room Tom got up and shook his friend's hand.

"Sorry I didn't greet you at the door, sport but I'm still feeling a bit below par," said Tom.

"No trouble at all. It's good to see you and thanks for inviting me for tea."

As they sipped the sherry that Martha had offered, Mike was apprised of his friend's illness and the necessity of him having to stay in a sanitarium for months.

"Sorry to hear that old boy," said Mike patting Tom's shoulder. "But I've heard they have lots of success in those places. Apparently, fresh air has a lot to do with it."

Just then Brian peeked around the door.

"Hello scallywag," said Mike. "Remember me?"

"Say hello to Mr. Williams Brian."

Brian came in and went over and this time he took Mike's hand to shake.

"Hello, Mr. Williams. Ma said your arm couldn't be sewn on."

"That's right son. It was too broken to fix but this arm is good and strong and comes in handy to tickle small boys like you," he said tickling Brian in the ribs and making him squirm with laughter.

"Stop!" yelled Brian. "No more."

"Alright no more for now, and you can call me Mike," he said taking another sip of sherry.

Janey came in then and after introductions and her polite response they all adjourned to the kitchen to partake of the cottage pie. During tea, the conversation centered on Attlee and the labour party however, Martha said she felt sorry for Churchill's loss as he had steered them through the tumultuous days of the war. Everyone agreed that the new NHS would be a great boon for the populace when it eventually got underway, although it was a shame that it was not covering the cost of Tom's treatment at the sanitarium.

Mike regaled them with some jokes he had heard in the office, although ensured that any risqué ones were withheld from the tender ears of the children present. She noticed Tom was not eating much as usual and prayed that they would be able to soon find the money for his treatment.

Tom asked how Mike's wife was and how long did she envisage she had to work after hours. He replied he wasn't sure as she had been rather non-committal on that score which left Martha wondering why she still had overtime work to do now that the war had ended.

"Da," said Brian.

"Yes, son."

"Are we going to the party on Saturday? You said if you feel alright, we could go."

"Let's just wait until Saturday," Martha said. "Would you like some more pie, Mike?" she added.

"Oh no, thanks, Martha. I think I have had an elegant sufficiency!" replied Mike.

Tom's glass remained empty of the stout that his friend had brought although Mike had offered him some as he poured his and Martha's. He had a sip of water and then as another cough overtook him became quite upset.

"God, bugger it all!" he shouted trying to extricate his handkerchief from his pocket but was too late to stop the drops of blood which fell to the floor.

Mike and Martha stood up and immediately went over to him as the children looked on aghast.

"There, there old sport," said Mike putting his arm around him.

"Leave me alone," he cried pulling away and heading for the stairs.

Martha went after him and calling over her shoulder thanked Mike for helping. She managed to get her husband into bed and after giving him a sedative and some comforting words went back down to her guest who was trying to clear the table. The children had fled to the sitting room and were listening to the wireless.

"Sorry about all that Mike," Martha said. "Here, I'll do this," she added taking Tom's plate of uneaten pie from him and scraping the remains into the bin.

"Don't mention it, Martha. Poor old fellow. How soon can he be admitted into the hospital?"

"Well, to be frank, it's as soon as we can find the money, I'm afraid Mike," said Martha as she put the kettle on.

"Oh, I see, well if I can contribute anything, just give me a shout," said Mike.

"That's very good of you, but we couldn't take your money. I am going to ring my mother tomorrow and see if she can help us."

"What about Tom's mother?" asked Mike. "Isn't she supposed to be well off?"

"Oh, she is but I'm afraid she refused Tom's request."

Mike raised his eyebrows and said, "Well, just remember what I said. Tom is a good fellow and the two of us have shared a lot through the war. I wouldn't like to let him down."

"I know Mike, and I really appreciate it, as I'm sure Tom would. Now, would you like a cup of tea, I know I could do with one at the moment!"

"Alright, only one. then I had better let you all have an early night."

"Well, go into the sitting room with the children and I will be with you shortly.

Mike went and found the children listening intently to a serial, their ears glued to the wireless. He sat down and taking the paper started leafing through it. Martha came with the tea and as they sat the sound of Tom's coughing assailed their ears.

"Martha, I was thinking, if Tom is not up to going on Saturday you could stay and look after him and I could take the children if you like."

"Oh, Mike that's nice of you. I really don't think he will be going the way he is at the moment."

Brian's ears picked up on the conversation.

"Can we go to the party then ma?" he asked excitedly.

"I think so pet, Mike has kindly offered to take you and Janey as I don't think your da will be well enough," said Martha.

"Is da's mouth bleeding ma?" asked Brian.

"Yes, darling it's all to do with his sickness."

Brian resumed listening to the program with his sister. his thoughts taken up with the upcoming street festivity which he had been looking forward to all week.

Tea finished, Mike stood up to take his cup and saucer into the kitchen.

"I'll take it, Mike."

"Thanks, Martha. Do you need help with the washing up?"

"No, it won't take me a minute. I'll get the children off to bed as it's a school night and then I will get stuck in."

"Oh, you're sure? I feel terrible leaving you to do all the work. Cooking the tea and everything."

"No, really, it's no bother. Thanks for coming Mike, and sorry it wasn't very pleasant."

"Thank you for inviting me. I hope the old boy feels better. Give him my regards and I will stop by to collect the children on Saturday."

"Alright, Mike that sounds good. I think if you come about eleven or so."

Martha called out to the children that Mike was leaving and to come and say goodbye.

"Bye Mike," said Brian and Janey.

"Bye youngsters, see you on Saturday," said Mike.

Martha farewelled her guest, closed the door, cajoled the children to bed, and then, after putting the kitchen to rights, stole upstairs to join her hopefully sleeping husband.

***

Harold quickly came waddling when he noticed Nora bringing his breakfast.

"Here you are then old fellow," she said as she emptied the scraps into the pen. "Enjoy."

***

Harold's snout was in the trough hoovering up his breakfast as though he had not eaten for a week.

"Greedy boy," said Nora as she gave his back a good scratch. "You like that, don't you?" Lucy came wandering over to see if there was anything for her.

"I haven't forgotten you, my girl," she said giving her the remains of the kitchen scraps.

As she did she heard the telephone ringing so, picking up the bucket she headed for the cottage, and taking off her wellingtons at the door padding inside.

"Hello," said Nora.

"Hello, mum?" said Martha.

"Oh, Martha dear. Is that you? I've been thinking about you. How are you all?" she asked settling down in her favourite chair.

"Oh, I'm alright and so are the children," replied Martha hearing the familiar click of the party line they shared with the neighbours, and hoping Ethel was not listening in to the call but knowing she probably was.

"And Tom?"

"Oh, mum," Martha started sobbing.

"What is it dear?"

"Tom isn't well. He has TB!"

"TB?"

"Yes, I took him to the doctor who sent him for an x-ray - he's been coughing blood!"

"Oh, Martha. I am sorry dear. He must have caught it in that camp or that horrible factory. Can he be cured?"

"Well, the thing is the doctor has told him he has to go to a sanitarium for six to nine months."

"A sanitarium, which one?" asked her mother.

"Well, apparently there are two. One is at a place called Brompton and the other one is at Frimley, and they are about 130 miles from London."

"That far?"

"Yes, it will take forever to get there."

"And what do these places charge?" asked Nora.

"That's the thing mum, they're not cheap. A private room at Frimley is 4 guineas and at Brompton, it's 5," said Martha blowing her nose and wiping her eyes.

"And we haven't got enough money to pay for it. Tom asked his mother, but she refused to give him anything."

"Well, that's typical of her! Now don't get all upset Martha," she said as she heard her sobbing "I have a bit of money put away. I was able to sell a few paintings at the market, so you just put your mind at rest and tell Tom to book himself into that place at Frimley."

"Oh mum, are you sure? You are so good. We will repay you when Tom is back on his feet."

"Don't worry about that. You just make sure he gets the best treatment. There is nothing as important as your health. I will send you a postal order to cash at the post office."

"Mum, you are the best!" exclaimed Martha filled with relief.

"Now, go and tell Tom not to fret anymore."

"I will, and thank you mum from the bottom of our hearts," cried Martha.

"I will ring you soon."

Nora put down the telephone and with a sigh made her way to the bedroom. Taking a key from under her mattress, she opened the bottom drawer of the dresser and pulled out an old tin of her husband's on the top of which was the insignia of the old Lyonesse steamship. Opening it, she counted out one thousand five hundred pounds which would be more than enough to cover her son-in-law's accommodation. Just as well I sold those paintings, she thought putting away the tin and locking the drawer. Money's no good if you can't spend it on something as worthwhile as this. It will do more good for Tom than for me. I don't want for anything and have all I need.

On a clod of unironed washing which was on the bed, she found a spot to sit. There her mind licked around the time when Martha was born and her dear Alistair had sailed off to fight for king and country, leaving her to bring up Martha on her own. Fortunately, she had been a good baby only becoming fractious whenever a new tooth was emerging from her gums.

Those times saw her in the arms of her mother in the old rocking chair being soothed back to sleep to the strains of a lullaby, while the Cornish waves slammed onto the rocks below. It proved to be mutually comforting and helped to distract Nora from thinking about her husband out on the broiling sea in the line of fire from the enemy.

Martha was a friendly, outgoing little girl who enjoyed school and the many friends she made were all welcomed back to the cottage on the cliff where Nora would have freshly baked scones to devour as after-school treats.

Many a day saw the old oak tree festooned with children as they either sat among the branches or swung on the seat from one of its boughs. Martha loved all their animals especially Billy the pig who would come snuffling along to the sound of her voice.

Showing an interest in dance, Nora enrolled her in a class held by an ex-ballerina called Madam La Touffe. With rouge daubed cheeks, hair pulled tightly back in a bun, and feet encased in ancient satin slippers, she had her young pupils enthralled as she chivvied them into plies and pas de deux, they all aspiring to be the lead role in The Nutcracker Suite or some other famous ballet.

Of course, all the local villagers knew that she was as French as they but as her teaching was quite excellent, nobody reproached her about it. Nora was so proud when she witnessed

2

her daughter perform in many concerts which were held in the local hall.

Through the years, mother and daughter had a close relationship, and on many days in the summer months, they could be found either swimming in the sea or picnicking on the sand, as Nora wielded her paintbrush and Martha sun-baked or read a book.

So, it was a sad day when Martha finally told Nora she had decided to test her wings and move to London. She had achieved good grades in her final exam at school and, as a test which she had sat, had shown an aptitude for office work, she had decided to enroll in a secretarial college.

Nora had been rather taken aback by this as she thought her daughter would lean towards more artistic pursuits, such as ballet or even painting as some of the sketches she had produced at school showed promise. However, as much as she would miss her company, she did not discourage but supported her decision to move away from Cornwall.

Although Martha knew she had to try for independence, it was in a mist of tears that she had boarded the train at Liskeard station, waving to her mother who had packed her a basket of homemade goodies to take on her journey.

She wrote to her mother about the boarding house in which she was living which housed many girls such as her, all unmarried and either studying or employed. She did not tell her about the dictatorial landlady who berated anyone who came in after hours or, heaven forbid anyone found to be entertaining the opposite sex in their room!

She did not tell her of the smells of boiled cabbage that permeated the building, tainting the very fabric of the curtains, or of the damp, together with the noises of the occupants next door, which seemed to seep through the thin walls of the establishment.

She did not tell her of the fellows she had met at various dances and smoky Soho bars, one fellow in particular who had wanted to come up to her room and complete the night with his bottle of ale, and her fending him off with the door slammed firmly in his face.

Nor did she ever tell her of the night she had been robbed of her purse at the bus stop and having to walk back in the pouring rain to her room which she had to access through a window with the help of her fellow boarders.

She certainly never told her of the married man whom she thought had loved her and to whom she had lost her virginity resulting in a pregnancy, about which he had not wanted to know. The consumption of large quantities of gin and hot baths taken in a vain attempt to rid herself of this unwanted baby all unsuccessful. Then the interview with the stern-faced nun at the convent of the sisters of St Joseph, where she would stay until the birth of her baby, ultimately to be given up for adoption.

No, these were things that Nora would never know as she would have summoned her daughter straight back to Polperro where she could keep a protective eye on her.

However, Nora was definitely told about the beautiful, kind man called Tom with whom she had fallen in love, who had made her heart sing and her life complete.

Her rumination completed; Nora walked into the kitchen where the sun was streaming in the window taking the morning chill with it. Looks like it will be a nice day for painting thought Nora as she turned on the wireless, from which emanated the sounds of Benny Goodman. Humming to the tune, she wielded the duster over the mantelpiece which held a plethora of knick-knacks. There was a collection of shells that she had gathered from the Scilly Isles and the little beach below her cottage, a toby jug, photos of Brian and Janey when they were babies, and other odds and ends that she always intended to put away but had not got around to.

She gave the floor a cursory sweep and then went into her little studio to collect her easel and painting requirements. Ensuring she had her key, she shut the door and headed to her favourite spot in the garden, where there was a collection of wildflowers and a view of the rocky cliffs. An oak tree offered shade in the summer months and Brian and Janey took great delight in climbing up into its branches when they came to stay. There was an old chair splashed with paint and, although it had seen better days, stood ready for occupation. Nora sat down and setting up her easel commenced to paint.

"Yoo hoo, are you there?" a voice shouted.

"Down here, in the garden," replied Nora.

Her friend, Meg approached bearing a plate of freshly baked scones.

"Hello, Meg. Been cooking again I, see?"

"Yes, these are fresh out of the oven, and they just need some of your blackberry jam and some clotted cream to make them worthwhile. But I can see you have just started painting. I can leave them for you to eat later on if you like," said Meg.

"No, they look too tempting and there is nothing like a freshly baked scone. We will have some now. The painting can wait."

Nora put her brush into the jar of turpentine and screwed the tops back on the paints and then the two friends made their way up to the kitchen.

Meg and Nora had been friends since school days and Meg's first husband had also been killed fighting in the battle of the Somme. Meg had met Kevin when he had come to Cornwall for a seaside holiday and as the relationship developed, they decided to marry, unlike Meg who had never found anyone to measure up to her dear Alistair.

"I'll put the kettle on and we'll have a nice cuppa," said Nora filling the kettle and placing it on the Aga.

Meg went to the dresser and took the plates, cups, and saucers and put them on the old, scrubbed kitchen table on which stood a jam jar filled with yellow daffodils. She then located a jar of blackberry jam.

"There should be some cream in the fridge, Meg," said Nora as she filled the teapot which was her favourite as it was the shape of a thatched cottage, and always looked cheerful sitting on the table.

"Ha found it!" said Meg.

"Good job I whipped some yesterday for the apple pie. I must have known you would be bringing scones today."

"Must have been mental telepathy," said Meg.

Martha poured the tea and they both helped themselves to the scones slathering on more than enough jam and cream than was good for them.

"I should be on a diet," announced Nora looking down at her rotund stomach. "I'm putting on too much weight. I shouldn't be hoeing into jam and cream like this."

"Fiddlesticks, we must start enjoying life now that the blooming war is over. If we can't enjoy some scones now we will never enjoy them. The diets can wait in my opinion!" said Meg as she helped herself to another scone.

"Well, what's news?" asked Meg.

"As a matter of fact, I had a call from Martha this morning," replied Nora taking a sip of tea.

"How is she?"

"Oh, she seems alright and so do the children. It's Tom that's the worry."

"What's happened?" Meg asked wiping some crumbs off her skirt.

"It appears he has TB. He saw a doctor who recommended he have an x-ray which confirmed it and he has to go to a sanitarium for treatment."

"Oh lord. That is bad news. Where does he have to go?"

"There is a place at Frimley which is about 130 miles from Ealing. I don't know how poor Martha is going to be able to visit him. It's such a long way."

"Yes, that's right," replied Meg. "Isn't there one a bit closer to them?"

"No, from what I gather these places are all a way out of London."

"I suppose it's to do with the fresh air they have to have. There wouldn't be much freshness in smoggy old London town," said Meg.

"How much will it cost them if you don't mind my asking?"

"No, I don't mind, Meg. It will be more than they can afford. Martha was so upset on the phone. I told her I would give them the money."

"You?"

"Yes, remember I sold those pictures a few weeks ago and made a tidy little profit. I would much rather Tom make use of it. He needs the money more than I do."

"Oh, Nora, you are so generous!" exclaimed Meg.

"Do you know if they asked the old witch of Belgravia?" she added.

Nora scowled. "Yes, apparently Tom put it to her but of course she refused. You wouldn't believe that a person like her, rolling in money could treat her own flesh and blood like that."

"Yes, she is a nasty piece of work alright. She will get her comeuppance one day and no mistake!" replied Meg.

"On a lighter note," added Nora, "are you and Kevin going to choir practice tomorrow night?"

"Yes, as far as I know. Are you?"

"Yes, I am. But I was wondering if the weather turns sour if it's not too much trouble, would you mind giving me a lift?"

"No trouble at all," replied Meg. "Just give me a ring and we will pick you up even if the weather is fine."

"Oh, if you're sure, that would be splendid. I should walk but my knee has been a bit sore lately. This old age doesn't have much to recommend it," said Nora.

"No, I agree with you there."

"Well, I'd better let you get on. Can't sit around nattering all day, much as I'd like to," said Meg rising from the table.

"Thanks for dropping in and thanks for those delicious scones, Meg," said Nora. "Don't forget your plate," she added quickly washing and drying it and giving it to her friend.

"Thanks, Nora, enjoy the rest of your day. Hope another masterpiece is in the making!" she said as she opened the door.

"I don't know about a masterpiece. Shall I ring you or will you pick me up?" she asked.

"We will come by around sevenish if that's alright?"

"That sounds perfect. I'll be ready. Thanks, Meg. Bye for now, enjoy your day, and thanks for popping in."

"Will do, bye," said Meg, and giving Nora a wave, she walked across the field and on to her cottage in the village.

Nora, after washing up the cups, saucers, and plates and putting them on the draining board went back outside to recommence her painting.

***

Martha, filled with relief knowing that her husband would now be able to receive the appropriate treatment due to the generosity of her mother, went straight to the sitting room to tell Tom the good news. She noticed the pallor on his face and thought the sooner he can be admitted to the sanitarium the better.

"Tom," she said as she sat down beside him and held his hand.

"Yes, darling."

"I have just been talking to mum and she is going to give us the money for your treatment. What do you think of that?"

Tom's eyes welled with tears and between coughing, he managed to gasp.

"I'm just a charity case. That's the truth of it. I have to rely on the charity of your mother!"

"No, Tom, don't be upset. Mum is only too happy to let us have the money. I told her we would pay her back when you are back on your feet."

"And when will that be I'd like to know?" Tom said wiping his eyes with his handkerchief which was stained with blood.

"When you have had your treatment and are recovered, Tom. Now, calm down and I will make us a nice cup of tea, then I will ring the doctor and tell him to book you in."

Martha went to the kitchen and after putting on the kettle went upstairs to the bedroom to fetch a clean handkerchief for her husband.

"Thanks, darling," he said as he swapped the dirty one for the clean one. "Sorry I got upset."

"That's alright, Tom. Now just relax and while the kettle is boiling, I will ring the doctor."

She went into the hall and dialled the number of the surgery.

"Doctor Burns' surgery, Annie speaking."

"Oh, hello, it's Mrs. Johnson speaking, Tom Johnson's wife. May I speak to the doctor please?"

"He is with a patient at the moment, Mrs. Johnson," replied the receptionist, "But I can ask him to ring you when he is free."

"Oh, yes, thank you if you wouldn't mind. It's rather urgent you see."

"Very well, what is your number?"

"It's Ealing 338."

"Thank you, Mrs. Johnson. The doctor will ring you as soon as possible."

Martha put down the phone and went to make the tea, praying that the doctor would not take long to ring her.

Handing Tom his cup she had just sat down when she heard the ring.

"Hello," Martha said.

"Hello, it's doctor Burns speaking. Is that Mrs. Johnson?"

"Yes, hello doctor. Thank you for ringing back."

"What can I do for you, Martha? How is your husband?" the doctor enquired

"Oh, doctor," Martha said her voice trembling. "I'm afraid he is not at all well. He is still coughing blood and today he has an awful pallor."

"Oh, I see. Well, it sounds as though he should be admitted as soon as possible. Have you decided anything about the sanitariums?"

"Yes, we have a doctor. We thought if you could book him into Frimley. That's the one which charges 4 guineas isn't it?" asked Martha.

"That's correct. He will have a private room. It's quite a nice place however, what it lacks in comfort it makes up for with excellent treatment. I have had patients admitted there over the years and their reports seemed favourable."

"Oh, that's good. I will tell Tom."

"Very well, I will ring them now and see if we can have him admitted tomorrow."

"Oh, that soon?" exclaimed Martha. "I had better start packing for him then. Does he need to take anything special?"

"No, just his usual clothes, pyjamas, a mackintosh, toiletries, and the like."

"I see. Well, thank you, doctor."

"I will ring you straight away when I have heard from Frimley," said the doctor.

"Alright, thank you," Martha said and putting the phone down thought about getting Tom's suitcase from the top of their wardrobe and giving it a good dust.

"Was that the doctor?" Tom asked as Martha came back to find that her tea had gone cold.

"Yes, dear. He said he would be contacting Frimley to see if you can be admitted tomorrow."

"Tomorrow?"

"Yes, so I had better start packing your suitcase. He said that Frimley has quite a good reputation as far as the treatment goes."

"Oh, well I hope they all recovered," said Tom despondently.

"I'm sure they did. Now, I had better sort out what you should take. Just as well the washing is up to date and your underwear dried," Martha said taking her cold tea into the kitchen and tipping it down the sink.

She thought how was Tom going to get to this place tomorrow and what about the children if she was to accompany him on the train? Maybe I can ask Ethel if she would mind them until she returned. Janey was quite mature and could look after her brother, but she did not yet want to put that sort of responsibility on her. She had quite a lot of homework to do now that she was going into senior school next year and Brian could be a little devil now and then. Yes, she would knock on the wall and talk to her neighbour.

"Ethel, sorry to bother you," Martha said after she had summoned her neighbour outside by knocking on the adjoining wall. "But I wonder could you do me a favour?"

"Any time, ducks what's the matter? You look worried like," said Ethel ashing her cigarette on the ground.

"Oh, Ethel, it's Tom. He has TB and might have to be admitted tomorrow to a sanitarium" explained Martha her eyes misting with tears.

"Oh, that's bad news and no mistake. I am sorry for you. Where is this place?"

"Well, this is the problem. It's quite a distance. About 130 miles away and if I go with Tom I don't know when I will be back. Could you watch the children for me? I could get Janey to look after Brian, but she has plenty of homework to do lately and I don't want to put too much responsibility on her."

"No, you can't do that, ducks. You just leave them with me. They'll be right as rain," said Ethel.

"Oh, are you sure? That would be so good of you Ethel. We're just waiting for the doctor to confirm the booking. I'll let you know when I hear anything."

"Oh, I can hear the phone now. Better go. Talk to you later." Martha dashed inside to answer the phone through which she heard that Tom would indeed be admitted to Frimley tomorrow.

Chapter Four

Set amidst well-groomed gardens and numerous pine trees, the grey building whose windows were all open to the elements, greeted Tom and Martha as they alighted from the taxi.

" 'Ere we are then, guv," said the driver as he opened the boot to retrieve Tom's suitcase and depositing it on the ground.

"That'll be two and sixpence."

Martha opened her purse.

"Thank you," she said.

Tom went to pick up the case but was stopped in time by an officious-looking matron who suddenly appeared and after whom hurried a frazzled porter trying his best to keep up.

"Good day," said the matron. "Don't you be carrying that," she admonished Tom. "George here will do it," pointing to the porter.

"Oh, thank you," Tom said to George as he did as he was told.

Matron addressed Tom "And you must be Mr. Johnson?"

"Yes, I am, and this is my wife Martha," said Tom breathlessly.

"Very well, follow me and we will get you settled." the matron commanded as she strode along leaving Tom, Martha, and the hapless George struggling with the suitcase in her wake.

"Now," said matron as they entered the foyer. "Sit yourselves down and we will get on with the paperwork."

They sat down.

She addressed George.

"Take Mr. Johnson's case up to room 16, there's a good man!"

George took the case and disappeared into an antique lift which seemed to take forever to go anywhere either up or down then with a rumble it eventually ascended with its cargo.

Matron put on her spectacles and commenced leafing through a large book.

"Ah, here we are," she announced. "Found you. It says you were referred by a doctor Burns of Uxbridge Road, Ealing, is that correct?" she addressed Tom.

"Yes, matron, that is right," answered Tom.

"Very good, and your full name is?" she asked her pen poised over the page.

"It's Thomas Andrew Johnson," said Tom.

"And what is your address?"

"79 Uxbridge Road, Ealing."

"And your date of birth?"

"19th January 1916."

"Next of kin?" she asked.

"It's my wife here, Martha."

Addressing Martha, she asked, "And what is your full name and date of birth Mrs. Johnson?"

"It's Martha Nora Johnson and my date of birth is 15th February 1914," Martha answered as she sat on the edge of her chair stealing a look at her husband and hoping he would be put to bed soon.

It had been quite a stressful day so far, starting with getting the children off to school and reminding them that Ethel was going to be looking after them when they returned. It had taken Tom a while to dress and shave, and they had arrived at the station with only minutes to spare.

She had mentally thanked her mother for the money which she had provided as some of it had gone on the taxis they were to be taking to and from the stations. There was no way they could have managed otherwise with Tom in such poor condition.

"Very good," answered the matron.

"And Tom," she added looking at him.

"Are you allergic to anything that you know of?"

Tom answered, "No I can't think of anything."

"And do you have children?" she asked.

"Yes," Martha interjected. "We have two, a boy and a girl. Janey is 12 and Brian is 5."

"Very good, well I think that is all the paperwork done, and here is the rule book for you to peruse which states that visiting hours are Thursday and Sunday 2 to 6 pm," the matron said as she removed her spectacles and stood up.

Martha cried, "Oh, can't I come at any other time? I have to travel a long way you see."

"I'm afraid the rules are the rules. We cannot have people traipsing in and out of here at all hours of the day. It would upset the patients' routine," she exclaimed.

"Now, if you will follow me I will take you to your room."

Martha, filled with angst stood up and helped Tom from the chair and they followed the matron into the lift. The door clanged shut and after what seemed like ages, with a jolt they suddenly ascended to the floors above.

They entered a room that was furnished with an iron bed, a chair, a small cupboard, and a table on which stood a jug of water and two glasses, one of which contained a thermometer. There was a sink, presumably for washing, and a small rug at the side of the bed provided a token of warmth, as the room was pervaded by a chill seeping through the open window. Martha thought how on earth was her poor sick husband going to get better here? He would probably catch pneumonia! She pulled her coat tighter around her trying to fend off the cold while Tom also buttoned his coat.

Noticing them the matron announced, "You probably are thinking why the window is open when it is so cold? Well, I'll tell you. We find that fresh air is the best remedy for tubercular patients. The more fresh air they have the better they will be."

"Now Tom," she added "I will leave you to unpack and then get yourself into bed. A nurse will be in shortly to take your temperature and so on. Goodbye."

And with that, she bustled from the room leaving Tom and Martha alone.

"Well," said Martha, "I had better do as commanded dear. You sit on the chair while I put your things away."

Tom, looking downcast, did as his wife suggested and as his coughing echoed in the room Martha quickly retrieved his flannelette pyjamas and helped him into them. She took a pair of woollen socks and put them on his damaged feet and then after he climbed into the bed, Martha ensured that the blankets were well pulled up to ward off the chill.

If only I could shut that blasted window she thought - it's freezing in here - but she had to put on a cheerful face for Tom's sake, so she tried not to think of the cold. The book he had brought she placed in the table drawer.

Just as Martha was closing the drawer a young cheerful nurse entered the room.

"Hello," she said brightly. "I am nurse Higgins."

"Pleased to meet you, I'm Martha," responded Martha. "And this is my husband, Tom."

"Well, hello Tom," said the nurse going over to the bed.

"Hello," murmured Tom.

"I am just going to take your temperature." She retrieved the thermometer from the glass and quickly placed it under Tom's tongue taking his wrist and commenced checking his pulse.

After a few minutes, the thermometer was removed, and the nurse announced Tom's temperature was up a bit, and then she proceeded to write something on the clipboard at the end of the bed.

Martha anxiously asked her, "Will he be alright?"

"No need to worry. We will keep an eye on him. I will bring him some aspirin which should help. Complete bed rest is what he needs now."

She addressed Tom, "Now Tom, would you like a cup of tea? I'm sure your wife would like one after that long journey on the train. I heard you came from Ealing?"

"Yes, that's right nurse," said Tom picking at the blanket. "And tea sounds very nice."

"Yes," added Martha. "I would love some too."

"Right you are then," said the nurse. "I shall have someone rustle you up a cup. Tea is at 5 pm."

"Thank you, nurse," Martha said, "And will Tom be having his meals in his room?"

"Yes, he will be eating in here."

"Oh, that's good," said Martha and addressing Tom "Isn't that good, Tom?"

"Yes, it is dear."

Martha then asked, "What time are the rest of the meals served, nurse?"

"Breakfast is at 5 am and lunch at 11:30 am, cocoa for supper around 7 pm and there is morning and afternoon tea served as well," replied the nurse as she poured some water from the jug into Tom's glass.

"I see," said Martha.

"Well, I'll go and see about your tea," the nurse said scurrying from the room.

Martha sat on the chair beside the bed and said brightly.

"Well, that all sounded rather good didn't it? All your meals brought in to you. You will feel like you are in a hotel having room service!"

Tom responded with a violent cough which resulted in a copious amount of blood being expectorated some of which had missed his handkerchief and had made its way onto the blanket.

"Oh, damn, and blast!" Tom cried.

"It's alright, dear. Don't worry. The nurse will clean it up when she comes back," Martha told him as she futilely attempted to rub at it with her handkerchief and some of the water from the glass.

The nurse came in then carrying a tray with two cups of tea, a jug of milk, a bowl of sugar, a plate of biscuits, and the aspirin.

"Here we are then," she said putting the tray on the table.

"Oh, nurse," said Martha "My husband had a little accident" she pointed to the red stain on the blanket.

"Oh, not to worry. This happens a lot around here. Comes with the territory you might say. I will tell one of the nurses to clean it for you," she said.

"Thank you," Martha said relieved. "And thank you for the tea."

"Oh," she added. "By the way, matron advised us that they are quite strict about the visiting hours here. I don't know how I am going to manage to come during those times as we live so far away."

The nurse winked, "Don't worry about what matron says about the rules. You can come any day between 3:15 and 5:15 pm when Tom is in bed."

"Oh, really? Thank you. That is a relief. I was worried how I was going to manage to bring the children and so on."

"Well," she said, "I'll leave you to enjoy your tea."

As the nurse exited the room Martha said to Tom.

"Thank goodness for that nurse Tom, she certainly put my mind at rest about visiting."

As Tom nodded, she handed him the aspirin and the glass of water which he swallowed slowly, then Martha stood up and poured the milk into the cups, adding some sugar to Tom's.

"Here you are, dear. A hot drink is just what you need."

"Thanks," said Tom taking the cup with shaking hands

"Just take a sip darling," she said making sure he did not spill any.

As she drank hers, she immediately felt the warmth soothing her body and her mind.

"There's nothing to beat a good cuppa!" she said to Tom who was having another sip.

"Do you want a biscuit?"

"No thanks. You have one. I think I will lie back and rest for a while."

"Alright then, you do that. You must be so tired. It's been a long day."

Martha took his cup and placed it on the table and then took a bite of a biscuit. Looking through the window she could see a few patients walking around the gardens. I wonder at what stage of recovery they are she thought. Oh god, she prayed, please make my Tom better so he can home to us and we all can have a normal family life.

She looked at her watch and to her shock, realised she had to leave if she was to catch the train which was due to leave at 3:30 pm.

"Tom," she whispered, "I have to go now."

"Oh," he said opening his eyes.

"Yes, dear. Now you try and have a rest and I will come and see you next weekend with the children, alright?"

"Alright," murmured Tom.

"Look after yourself and do what the nurses tell you."

"I will."

"I love you, Tom," Martha whispered, her lips brushing his.

"Love you too," he whispered back.

Martha took her bag and with tears coursing down her cheeks left the room and the sanitarium to make her way back to Ealing.

The seething train was at the station when Martha alighted from the taxi and she still had to buy her ticket. There were a few people in front of her and she wished they would hurry. There was a woman who was having an interminable dispute with the cashier about the price of the fare.

"But surely it can't be that much," she railed. "It's daylight robbery, that's what it is!"

"Madam, you either pay the fare or you don't travel. There are people behind you waiting. So, make up your mind, are you going to pay or not?" the cashier asked her wiping his brow with all the stress.

"Well, no need to be rude. I'll give you the money but mark by words, sonny, I'll not be travelling much more!" she exclaimed throwing the money down and taking her ticket stomped off to board the train.

Oh lord, thought Martha, I hope she won't be sitting next to me!

"Next," said the cashier, and the man in front of her moved up, and soon she had bought her ticket and secured a seat fortunately not next to the belligerent woman.

Looking through the window as the train picked up speed, Martha's mind was filled with thoughts of her poor Tom shut away in that cold, bleak building. Dear god, she prayed again, please make Tom better and don't let him be cold especially at night when he felt the cold more than ever, and he doesn't have me to keep him warm. Tears again ran unchecked down her checks as the train took her further away from her husband.

The woman sitting opposite noticed her distress and excusing herself said.

"Are you alright, dear? Can I help?"

"Oh no, thank you. I'll be alright in a minute," replied Martha blowing her nose on her handkerchief.

"Have you had bad news?" she asked.

"It's my husband, you see," said Martha wiping her eyes. "I have just left him at the Frimley sanitarium. He has TB."

"Oh, I am sorry for you dear. But those places have a good success rate if that's any consolation."

"As a matter of fact, my nephew is one of the doctors there so he might be treating your husband."

"Oh, really?" Martha exclaimed. "That would be a coincidence wouldn't it?"

"Yes, it would. His name is Edward, Edward Young. You tell your husband to look out for him."

"Oh, yes I will, thank you," replied Martha.

Her travelling companion put her hand into her basket and drew out a sandwich which she then offered to Martha.

"Oh, thank you. I haven't eaten anything since this morning except for a biscuit at the hospital," said Martha as she unwrapped the sandwich and took a bite.

"How did he get TB?" the woman asked as she also attacked a sandwich.

"He was a prisoner of war and he was made to work in one of the factories in Germany," said Martha.

"Oh, what was the factory?" she asked.

"It was the Siemens factory and apparently it was near that place called Ravensbruck where the women were imprisoned.

"Merciful heaven!" she gasped "That was a shocking place, so I heard."

"Yes, it was. Tom my husband, told me that some of the women were sent back and forth from there to the factory and they were in a terrible state."

"Poor souls! Those rotten Germans!" she exclaimed "The suffering they have caused. I hope they all rot in hell!""

"Have you any children dear?" she asked changing the subject to something a little lighter as the train went through a tunnel pitching them into darkness.

"Yes, two. A boy and a girl," answered Martha.

They were out of the tunnel but now the daylight was drawing to a close and Martha hoped she would be home before it was completely dark.

"That's lovely for you. I only had one child and he was killed in France."

"Oh, I'm sorry," said Martha.

"Yes, it's hard. I have just been visiting my sister in Frimley. The one whose son is the doctor. Her other boy was also killed in the same battle as my Nevil. They had enlisted together you see. Millicent has taken it hard. She always had a nervous disposition and losing her Jeffrey really set her back. If she only had something to occupy her, take her mind off things, she would be better off," she ventured.

"Yes, it must be terrible for you all. I suppose I should be grateful that at least Tom is still alive, even though he is ill. Was your nephew, the doctor, in the war?" asked Martha.

"Yes, he was in the medical corps in one of the clearing stations and from what I can gather he had to deal with some horrific injuries but thank heavens he came home unscathed."

"He was very fortunate," said Martha as she finished the sandwich.

"That's right dear, he was. But now we must look to the future and treasure every day. We only miss things when they're not around anymore."

The train was entering the outskirts of London and Martha was aware that it wouldn't be long until she was at her station.

"I'm getting off soon," she said, "By the way, my name is Martha."

"And I'm Joan. It was lovely to meet you, dear."

"Yes, it was, and thank you so much for the sandwich. It kept me going until I have tea tonight. Where are you getting off?" she asked.

"Haven Green."

"Oh, right. I might bump into you one day at the shops then," said Martha standing up and getting ready to alight as the train slowed down.

"Yes, you never know. I am forever bumping into people I know."

"Well, goodbye Joan, and thanks again for your company," said Martha leaving the compartment.

"Goodbye Martha and take care of yourself, dear," replied Joan.

Chapter Five

Tom looked at the ceiling his eyes blurred by tears. He was already missing his darling wife and children and thought how was he to cope closeted away in this place of sickness for months on end. He thought about his life before he met Martha.

He had been mainly brought up by nanny Philpott as his father, being involved with new developments in the railways, was absent most of the time. His mother, when she was not accompanying her husband on overseas voyages, had been occupied with her society friends, either at cocktail parties or endless luncheons at the Ritz or the Savoy. He was sent to a prep school and then, at the behest of his mother, had ultimately been enrolled at Cambridge.

When he came of age, his mother had wrangled an invitation to a country house weekend in the Scottish Highlands where she thought he would be introduced to some eligible daughters of the landed gentry, and hopefully fall in love with one of them, but to no avail. He had found those girls so vacuous and mercenary with not very much to talk about, apart from in which chateau they would be holidaying, or to which ball they would be attending, that he had been glad to see the back of them. Also, as he did not shoot, he had found himself on the periphery with the beaters and the ruddy-faced factor, whose conversation centred on the financial affairs of the estate, and the poor condition of the gatehouse in which he resided.

Annette Creswell

The obsequious butler had only added to his misery by criticising him for not bringing his own valet for the weekend stay. "It is not the done thing!" he had remonstrated as Tom told him he could manage without one, and he had swanned off in an attempt to purloin lord Shelby's valet to step into the breach.

When the weekend finally ended, and he was on his way on the train back to Cambridge, he vowed to himself that he would not accept another invitation to any more country house weekends no matter how much his mother protested. He felt like a square peg in a round hole, not fitting in.

He had contracted glandular fever during the third term which had resulted in him missing a lot of tutorials. Exams failed; he was ultimately sent down. His mother had of course blamed the "ordinary" girls with whom he kept company for giving him the virus, as she had said that girls of the upper class would not be harbouring such germs!

He then enrolled in the London School of Economics, much to his mother's chagrin and to a lesser extent his father's, and managed to obtain his degree in accountancy which enabled him to apply for the position at the Cunard shipping office in which Mike Williams was also employed.

The night he had met Martha he had been asked to play the saxophone at a dance at Bournemouth as the regular musician was ill. He had learnt to play when he was at Cambridge but had been forced to give it up by his mother as she felt he was not devoting enough time to his studies. The instrument was thus relegated to the cupboard in his rooms and only taken out to be played on occasions.

Martha, who was a legal secretary, had come for a holiday with her friend Helen with whom she had been sharing a flat, and they decided to attend the dance. Helen was a nurse and she had invited Martha to share her flat as her former flatmate had decided to move out.

He had noticed Martha straight away as her shiny brown hair swung around to the beat of the music, eyes alight with joie de vivre. During a break, Tom had walked over and with all the courage he could muster, introduced himself and asked if she wanted a drink. He was rewarded with her disarming smile and an acceptance of a gin and it.

Throughout the night, in between the breaks, they had managed to talk and Tom had obtained her permission for him to see her again when they both returned to London. After a suitable time of courting, when they discovered they had lots in common, such as liking the same films, enjoying the beach and the great outdoors, and just being together in companionable silence, not feeling to have to talk all the time.

Then one day with a picnic basket filled with cheese, bread, strawberries, and a bottle of merlot they had climbed to one of their favourite places high on Bodmin moor. It was there on a rocky outcrop with the wind tugging at their clothes, that Tom had asked his precious girl to marry him. In the ancient ivy-clad church in Polperro in which Martha had attended services as a child, their union was blessed.

Tom's mother had come under sufferance as she had wanted him to marry somebody more upper class than Martha. She would have loved a notice posted in the Times advising that her son was to be betrothed to Lady such and such of such and such and lording it over all her snooty friends!

At the wedding, she had spoken only perfunctorily to Martha's mother Nora. Looking down her nose at her rather bucolic attire, she had flounced around in pearls and satin, wearing a hat that would have been suitable for a royal wedding in Westminster Abbey! Nora had been the complete opposite of

Sylvia and Tom, enveloped in her warm-hearted and friendly nature, had taken to her at first introduction.

Tom thought of their honeymoon at Penzance. They had spent their days walking hand in hand over the beach looking into the rockpools for any little sea creatures they could find and went rambling over the moors stopping at cosy cafes where over Cornish teas they would indulge in mutual repartees.

Then, after dining in front of a roaring fire, they would retire to their room there to enjoy the delights of wedded bliss, as their bodies merged together as one. Oh, Tom thought, how he would love to have those moments again but now all he had were memories. My Martha does not deserve to be living with only half a man he thought. I cannot be what a husband should be. God, bugger the war and bugger this disease! Maybe I should have done what mother had wanted me to and not gone at all. Just stayed at home, been ostracised, and given white feathers. It might have been better than all this.

He was brought suddenly back from his reminiscences as a nurse came in with a tray.

"Here is your tea," she said placing the tray on the table, and was gone without another word uttered, the blood stain still left on the blanket.

Tom found a plate of cold roast beef and potatoes accompanied by a bowl of jelly and custard. Desultorily he picked at the salad but then decided to have some custard. He thought of his family at home seated at the table in the kitchen and another tear escaped down his cheek.

Nurse Higgins entered the room "Hello Tom" she said, "Have you tried to eat some tea?"

"Oh, I had a little custard" replied Tom brushing away the wetness from his face and hoping the nurse had not noticed his distress.

"Well, that is better than nothing," she said breezily. "The main thing is to drink plenty of fluids. Would you like a cup of tea or wait for the cocoa to come around later?"

"I think I will wait for the cocoa thanks."

She straightened the cover, "Very good. Your wife seemed nice."

"Yes, she is."

Noticing his despondence, she said reassuringly, "You'll soon get used to this place, Tom. The first day is always the hardest. Like starting a new job."

"Yes, I suppose it is."

"Well, have some cocoa later. It should help you sleep, and I will look in on you before lights out"

"Alright, thank you nurse."

Tom hoped that what the nurse said was true. That he would get used to this place and he tried to think positively and to look forward to the times when he would see his beloved wife again. He took the book from the drawer and tried to read but soon thoughts of the camp and the factory intruded rendering the endeavour useless. There was nothing for it but to wait until the cocoa arrived to hopefully put an end to this interminable day.

***

Martha had arrived home later than she had expected. Ethel had kindly given them some tea albeit baked beans on toast, which Brian liked as it meant he did not have to eat his vegetables. Janey was doing her homework, and Brian was listening to the wireless with Ethel when Martha came in the door.

"Hello," she cried.

Brian ran out to her, "Ma, you're back."

"Yes, pet ma's back now. I thought I would never get here. I hope you have been a good boy for Ethel?"

"Oh, yes, he has and so has his sister" interjected Ethel as she came from the sitting room.

"Oh, Ethel, thank you so much for looking after them. Sorry, I'm so late" Martha said taking off her coat and hanging it on the rack.

"It wasn't any bother, ducks. We had a good time, didn't we boyo?" said Ethel patting Brian on the head.

"And how is Tom?" she asked.

Janey came flying down the stairs.

"Hello ma, what is the hospital like? Does da like it?"

"Well, I was just going to tell Ethel. Da has his own room and is settling in. There is a nice nurse looking after him and he is going to be able to eat his meals in his room just like being in a hotel!" she explained trying to sound optimistic.

"Can we see him soon?" asked Brian.

"Yes, we will go next weekend, probably on Sunday."

"That's good, 'cause the party is on Saturday and Mike said he will take us didn't he ma?"

"Yes, he did darling."

Ethel said, "Now let your ma have some peace. I will boil the kettle for a nice cuppa."

The children ducked off to their respective interests.

"Oh Ethel, that sounds nice. It's just what I need."

"You just sit yourself down then, Martha. After such a long day you've had, you must be just about all in!"

"Yes, you could say that. I feel quite exhausted."

Martha took Ethel's advice and sat down. The headache which had been threatening since she left the hospital had now become fully blown. Ethel grilled some toast and heated the rest of the beans and, after making the tea, poured a cup for herself and Martha.

"Oh, thank you, Ethel that is good," said Martha as the hot liquid made its way down her throat.

Ethel passed her the beans on toast, and it did not take long for it to be devoured.

"Well," said Ethel. "Did Tom settle in alright? With the youngsters around suppose you didn't want to say much."

"Oh Ethel, the place was so cold. I couldn't bear it and with Tom so sick."

"There, there lovey," said Ethel patting her arm as tears began to fall.

"I heard those places have to have a lot of fresh air through them. Get rid of the germs like!"

"Yes, I know, but I hated to leave him there like that. He feels the cold so much Ethel, especially at night," she cried.

"Now don't go worrying about him. He is in the best of hands, you mark old Ethel's words, ducks!"

"Oh, I pray he is Ethel, and he will get well and come home to us."

Ethel assured her that would be the outcome and after calling goodbye to the children she let herself out and went in next door to have another well-earned cigarette.

Martha finished her tea and, putting everything in the sink with the intention of washing it in the morning, went upstairs to put herself and the children to bed.

With a pounding head, she lay awake for a while thinking over the events of the day. It had been so physically and mentally draining escorting poor sick Tom on the train as he coughed and expectorated into his handkerchief, to the chagrin of the other passengers as they looked at him aghast. One man attired in a pinstripe suit had even got up off his seat and, taking his briefcase from the rack above, stalked out of the compartment with a look of complete disdain on his face.

Martha had felt so embarrassed and hoped that nobody knew that Tom had TB. She was so relieved when the train had stopped at Frimley, and they were at last able to get off and into a taxi that drove them straight to the sanitarium.

Thank heavens for my neighbour, Ethel she thought. Although she was a busy body, she had a good heart and would help anyone in their time of need. With that final thought, Martha drifted off into a dreamless sleep, until the alarm sounded announcing another day to be faced without her darling husband beside her.

Chapter Six

The first fingers of sunshine sneaked through the curtains and Brian jumped out of bed and ran to his sister's room.

"Wake up Janey," he said poking her through the blanket.

"Go away, Brian, go back to bed. It's too early," moaned Janey pulling the blanket further over her head.

"But it's Saturday, Janey and the party is on today," cried Brian.

"I know, but it doesn't start until after 11 o'clock. Go back to bed and let me sleep!"

Disappointed that his sister was not going to join him in his excitement, he decided to go downstairs and see what he could find to eat before his mother made their breakfast. He pushed a chair towards the cupboard and reached for the biscuit tin. He had just managed to grab a handful when in walked his mother.

"Brian," she said. "You know you shouldn't be eating biscuits before breakfast. Put those away."

"Yes, ma," said Brian as he threw the pilfered biscuits back into the tin.

"What are you doing up so early, pet?" said Martha as she filled the kettle to make a cup of tea.

"It's the party today, ma!"

"Yes, but it won't be starting until later."

"That's what Janey said."

"I hope you didn't wake her," said Martha. "She likes to have a sleep-in on Saturday."

Brian looked sheepish and looked down at the floor not wanting to admit that he woke his sister.

Martha filled the teapot and asked Brian if he would like some porridge.

"Yes, please," he said. "Ma, is Mike still taking us to the party?"

"Yes, pet he is," said Martha stirring the porridge. "I will come for a while. but I thought I would go and see my friend Helen and her mum and you and Janey can stay with Mike. How would that be?"

"Alright, but I wish da could come too," Brian said as he played with the spoon pushing it around the table.

"I know darling, but we are going to see him tomorrow and we will be going on a long train ride. That will be good won't it?"

"Will we see any animals on the way?"

"Yes, probably. There should be some sheep. You and Janey can play a game and the one who sees the most will win!"

"What will we win ma?"

"I'll think of something," Martha said as she spooned the porridge into a bowl and gave it to her son.

"Can I have some brown sugar?"

"Only a little. You always put too much on Brian."

Martha took the bowl of sugar from the cupboard and put it on the table and watched as Brian put the minimum amount onto the porridge. Then he stirred it around and took a mouthful.

"Too hot!" he cried spitting it back into the bowl.

"Well, wait til it cools a bit silly billy," said Martha sitting down and taking a mouthful of tea.

Janey came in.

"Good morning darling. Did you have a good sleep?" asked Martha.

"Yes, I did until Brian woke me up," answered Janey quite put out.

"Brian!" admonished Martha.

"Well, I forgot it was early ma," said Brian stirring the porridge around and around.

"Well, don't wake me up that early again, Brian, especially on Saturday," said his sister sitting down and sprinkling sugar on her porridge.

"Janey," said Martha.

"Yes, ma."

"I was just telling Brian I might see my friend Helen and her mum today. I will come to the party for a little while and then go. Mike will be there with you."

"Alright," said Janey.

They finished their breakfast and Martha went to the sink to be confronted with last night's dirty plates which she had forgotten about. As she washed up her thoughts strayed to how her poor Tom was faring and she was glad she would be again seeing him tomorrow.

The morning passed and before long a knock sounded on the door and there was Mike ready to accompany them to the party. The foursome walked up the street with Brian in the lead champing at the bit to be the first arrival. Trestle tables groaning with food had been set up along the road, while an assortment of colourful bunting and flags hung from the telegraph poles. A salvation army brass band added to the party atmosphere.

Brian made for the iced cupcakes, and before Martha had a chance to stop him, he had stuffed one into his mouth and had another in his hand ready to be devoured. As Martha placed her contributed plate of sandwiches on one of the tables, she noticed Janey talking to her friend Mary. She was with her mother guarding a perambulator in which lay a rosy-cheeked baby boy.

Martha had told Mike of her plan to see her friend Helen a little later, and he had told her he would be only too glad to keep an eye on the children. He did not seem his usual cheerful self and, when Martha had asked about his wife, he changed the subject. Martha wondered if all was well with his marriage but refrained from asking any questions so as not to embarrass him.

She spoke to the neighbours whom she knew, everyone asking after Tom and sending him their warm wishes for a speedy recovery. There were a few returned soldiers in the crowd who, like Mike, had various afflictions, and legacies of the war. The ones whose legs were missing were being pushed in wheelchairs by their stoic wives all ensuring their husbands were not missing out on any of the cheer.

After they had eaten some sandwiches and had a cup of tea, Martha told Mike she would leave. She went over to Brian who was sitting on the road playing marbles with one of his schoolmates.

"Brian, pet," she said as she hunkered down with him. "I am going now. Be a good boy for Mike and go home when he tells you."

"Alright," said Brian sending a blue marble skittering across the ground.

"And don't eat any more cakes please, otherwise you will have a tummy ache and I don't want you ill tomorrow when we have to see your father," she added standing up and looking around for Janey.

She spotted her talking to Mary and after telling her she was leaving thanked Mike for looking after the children then set off for Helen's house.

Helen lived only a few blocks away so it did not take Martha long to arrive.

She knocked on the door.

"Martha," exclaimed Helen. "Great to see you, come in."

Martha entered and followed her friend into a bedroom where her mother Val was sitting up in bed. A pink crocheted bed jacket adorned her shoulders and Martha could see that her hair had been recently washed and brushed by her daughter in anticipation of Martha's visit. The room was spick and span, the floor gleamed with polish and there was a vase of daisies on the table next to the bed. A bookcase replete with books added to the cosiness of the room. Martha could see that dear Helen was doing an excellent job caring for her mother and hoped that she would someday have the favour returned and receive the happiness to which she was due.

"Hello Val," said Martha sitting down in the chair and taking her hand being rewarded with a smile.

Helen said, "Isn't it good to see Martha's mum?"

Another smile crossed Val's face and she gave a perceptible nod.

"Come into the kitchen Marth, while I make us some tea," said Helen.

"Alright, see you shortly Val," Martha said as she followed Helen into the kitchen.

"Oh, it's so good to see you," exclaimed Helen. "Sit down and tell me all the gossip."

Martha sat down and as Helen put the kettle on she commenced regaling her friend of all her news, in particular, Tom's admission into the sanitarium.

"I wouldn't worry too much about Tom, Marth. I'm sure he will get the best treatment where he is" said Helen as she took the cups and saucers and placed them on the tray.

"I know Helen, but I can't help it. I think I will feel more reassured when I see him again tomorrow."

"Yes, that's right, it will take getting used to I imagine. How much do these places cost?" she asked now cutting a cake which she had obviously made for the occasion.

"It's not cheap. We had to ask mum for a loan."

"Oh."

"Yes, I had to ring and ask her, as of course Tom's mother refused point blank."

"Typical!"

"You've said it. That woman will be the death of me the way she treats Tom. It's disgusting."

Helen nodded in acknowledgment.

"And did your mum agree to lend you some?"

"Yes, she did thank heavens. Apparently, she sold some paintings which fetched good prices. I told her we would pay her back when Tom gets back on his feet but she wouldn't hear of it"

"Well, you are certainly lucky to have such a generous mum. She makes up in spades for the skinflint."

Helen assembled everything and she and Martha went back to Val whose eyes were now closed but as she heard movement in the room became alert and looking at the cake on the tray became more animated.

"Here we are then, mum. I think you would like a slice of cake, wouldn't you?" Helen asked as she set down the tray and proceeded to feed her mother morsels of cake.

Martha drew up the other chair and helped herself to a piece of cake and the tea.

"Martha was telling me about the street party which is on today," Helen told her mother as she held the cup to her mother's lips so she could sip.

"Yes" interjected Martha "The salvos' band was playing all the old tunes which you used to like and there were union jacks and bunting hung from the telegraph poles."

Val's face lit up and Martha felt so sorry for this poor woman cooped up in bed for months on end who was unable to talk or feed herself, unable to partake of the life that she, Martha enjoyed. She thought there was always someone more unfortunate than herself and she must learn to enjoy life while she was able even though she was finding it hard at the moment with Tom so sick. Even dear Helen always seemed cheerful as she cared for her mother to the detriment of her own enjoyment.

As they were finishing their tea, they heard a knock on the door.

Helen went to answer it and Martha thought she heard Brian wailing.

She put down her cup and hurried out and there were Mike, Janey, and Brian with a freshly skinned knee crying for his mother.

"Oh, Brian what have you done now?" she asked going over to him.

"I fell over and hurt my knee again" he cried.

Mike interrupted.

"Sorry I had to barge in like this, but he was in such a state and only wanted you. Janey directed us here and, well I'm afraid, here we are."

Martha quickly introduced Helen to Mike and apologised for the intrusion.

"Oh, it's no problem really. As a matter of fact, it's good to have some visitors. Come into the sitting room, everybody. I'm sure there is some cake left over."

"Oh, don't go to any trouble," Mike said feeling like a trespasser "I can go and leave you all to it now the children are safe."

"No, don't be silly. You are most welcome," said Helen

Everybody trooped in and Helen and Martha bustled off with Brian who had quietened down a bit so his knee could be washed, and iodine applied.

"I don't know Brian; you are always in scrapes," said Martha as she dabbed at his knee much to his consternation.

"It was an accident, ma," he said sniffling.

"I can't leave you for two minutes," she added. "Job done." Helen then told them to join the others and she would tell her mother what was happening.

She came back with the leftover cake which was immediately set upon by Brian to the protestation of his mother and Helen said she would make them some more tea.

Janey asked if she could look in on Val and Helen said she was sure her mother would love it.

While they were gone, Martha told Mike about her friendship with Helen caring for her bed-ridden mother to which he listened with interest and much sympathy for her plight.

The cake devoured by Brian was an antidote for his sore knee and it wasn't long before he was whining to go home.

Helen asked Mike.

"Would you like to say hello to mum before you go?"

"Yes, Helen, I would love to," said Mike.

He followed her into Val's room.

"Mum, this is Mike, Tom's friend. They fought in the war," she explained.

Val's face lit up again and Mike gave her a little wave.

His eyes alighted on the bookcase and going over he noticed there were some first editions of Dickens' books.

He asked Helen "Are they your mum's?"

Helen replied "Yes, they are. Mum used to be rather a bookworm but as her eyesight has deteriorated, she cannot manage now. I read to her when I can but lately, I don't seem to have much time."

"Oh, well, as a matter of fact, I must confess that I am known to have my head in a book more than I should, and when I was convalescing in the hospital, I used to read to the chaps who weren't able, you know, blinded and so on," he said.

"If it's not an imposition, I could come over now and then and read to her if you like," he added.

"Oh, really, that would be excellent. But are you sure? You must have other things to do," Helen said overcome that he had suggested such an idea.

"No, it would be my pleasure. I seem to have spare time lately, especially after work and it would make me feel useful," said Mike.

"That would be wonderful, thank you," said Helen.

"What times would suit you? I finish work at 4 pm so I could be here around 4:30 pm."

"That would be perfect. It would give me a chance to make the tea."

"Well, that's settled. What say I come on Monday and give it a tryout? If I'm not up to your mother's expectations she can always give me the flick!"

"I don't think she would do that, Mike. I think you would make her day and give her something to look forward to."

Mike said goodbye to Val with the promise that he would be back in a couple of days to read to her which made her eyes crinkle with happiness.

Martha and the children were already at the door ready to leave when Mike and Helen joined them.

"I'll just dash and say goodbye to Val," said Martha.

She returned, and saying farewell to her friend and thanking her for her hospitality to everyone, she and Mike with the children all set off for Uxbridge Road. They had not gone far when to her surprise Mike announced that he intended to visit Helen's mum and read to her in his spare time. This comment reinforced Martha's suspicion that things were not well at home.

Chapter Seven

It was Monday and yesterday Martha had taken the children on the train to see their father at Frimley. They had left the house in the pouring rain and Martha was pleased that they all had their wellingtons. Brian kept complaining about his sore knee and Martha and Janey had to cajole him to hurry up or they would miss the train. Fortunately, there was no queue at the ticket office so they boarded the train without further delay.

They had just settled into a compartment when a rotund ruddy-faced man encumbered by a huge suitcase and a basket out of which poked the head of a cat, squeezed his way in. Putting the basket on the seat, he manoeuvred the case onto the rack with some difficulty then with a sigh plonked himself down on the seat.

"Mornin," he said.

"Good morning," replied Martha.

"Is that your cat?" asked Brian looking into the basket.

"Yer, that's me cat alright young'un," said the man.

"What's its name?" asked Brian.

"He's called Mugsie. Do ya want to pat 'im?"

Brian reached over to pat the cat but it let out a hiss and bared its claws.

"I don't think you should disturb the cat, pet," said Martha worried that it would scratch her son and thought it would be just his luck to catch some feline disease to add to her worries.

Janey had commenced reading her book, The Magic Faraway Tree, and was rather disinterested in the arrival of their travelling companion.

The man piped up.

"Where you goin'?"

Martha replied, "We are going to Frimley."

"Yes," Brian said, "We're going to see our da in the hospital."

"Oh, are ya now? And what's wrong with your da?"

"He has BT," said Brian.

"BT is it?" said the man whose cat was now crawling out of the basket and onto the seat.

"Haven't 'eard of that one sonny," he said grabbing Mugsie who yowled in protest as he was put back into the basket.

"But I've 'eard of TB. Is that what your da has?"

Martha interjected. "Yes, it is."

"Oh, well my cousin had that, and he were so sick he 'ad to 'ave an operation."

"Oh," said Martha not wanting to hear anymore so changing the subject she asked.

"And where are you going?"

"I'm on me way to the brother's farm," he told her.

"Why?" asked Brian wanting to know all details.

"'Cause I'm goin' to live with 'im. Me and Mugsy."

"Why are you doing that?" asked Brian.

"Brian," said Martha. "Don't ask so many questions, it's rude."

"Young'un's alright," said the man.

"I'm goin' 'cause I can't afford to stay in London," he said "Gov'mint is pulling down me 'ouse and I don't want to go to one of 'em fancy places. Rather live in country where I were born."

Brian's curiosity satisfied, he took a sandwich from his mother and tried to look through the window which had misted with the rain. Martha offered Janey and the man a sandwich, the latter pouncing and devouring it as if he hadn't eaten in a week. Martha was feeling sorry for the fellow, being uprooted from his home and obviously short of money.

"Yer," he continued. "I were born on Christmas Day when it were that cold it would freeze the balls of a brass monkey and no mistake! Me poor ma 'ad me in the bed as the old midwife couldn't get through all the snow and me da caught me as I popped out!" he told them now clearly enjoying himself.

Brian asked, "Where did you pop out from?"

"From me ma, sonny."

Martha interjected. "Would you like another sandwich Mr...er."

"Name's Potter, Alfie Potter."

"Nice to meet you, Mr. Potter. This is Brian," and, pointing to Janey.

"That is Janey and I'm Martha," she said as the offered sandwich went the way of the former.

He continued, "I 'as nine brothers and two sisters 'tho only three is still livin'"

"Oh," said Martha in astonishment "That's a big family!"

"That's right missus. They 'ad big families in the old days. Nothin' much to do at night but 'ave a bit of the old slap and tickle if ya know what I mean!" he guffawed which startled the cat who nearly jumped out of the basket again.

To Martha's relief, the train had pulled into the station so bidding goodbye to the garrulous Mr. Potter, Martha and the children stepped out of the train and into a waiting taxi which whisked them away to the sanitarium.

When they entered the room Tom was lying down with no discernible improvement in his pallor. A nurse was just completing some notes on the chart at the end of the bed.

"Hello dear," said Martha going over and kissing his cheek "I've brought the children to see you" and coaxing them to come closer to their father she said.

"Say hello to your da then."

"Hello, da" they chorused.

The nurse drew Martha aside and told her that Tom was going to need an artificial pneumothorax and the operation was scheduled in three days time. She assured her it would not be a major operation but would be carried out under a local anaesthetic. She then said she would bring in a couple more chairs and dashed to locate some.

"Thanks for coming darling" croaked Tom.

Brian was trying to read what the nurse had written on the chart but as he could not decipher anything went over to the open window. He tried to close it but Janey admonished him.

"Brian, leave the window alone. Da has to have it open."

"But it's cold in here" whined Brian.

"Yes, but da has to have the fresh air so he can get better. Isn't that right ma?" asked Janey.

"Yes, pet, that's right. Now, come over here Brian."

The nurse came in carrying two chairs on which Janey and Brian sat while Martha went over and sat on the one next to the bed.

"So, the nurse told me you have to have a little operation?" she said holding her husband's hand, shocked to find it felt thinner than last time.

Tom replied, "Yes, they told me this morning. It involves collapsing the affected lung and after that, I have to lie flat for a day with one pillow, then the next day two."

"Will it hurt da when they clapse your lung?" asked Brian.

"No, son," whispered his father who seemed tired by the effort of speaking.

"Da will have an anaesthetic so he will not feel any pain, pet."

"Oh, that's good," said Brian who was now in the process of picking his nose.

"Brian," said his sister "I wish you wouldn't do that. It's disgusting! Use your hanky"

"Haven't got one," he said sulkily.

"Here, use mine," said Martha.

He took his mother's embroidered hanky and proceeded to poke it into his nose then mission accomplished, gave it back to her.

Tom's eyes had closed so Martha decided she would take the children to have a look around the grounds. They boarded the ancient lift which still took an age to move and eventually deposited them on the ground floor. They went through the door and outside where now the rain had stopped, leaving the leaves on the trees still dripping droplets of water. The puddles on the ground delighted Brian who jumped into them, sending sprays of mud flying everywhere.

"Stop that Brian, get out of those puddles" Martha cried "You will have us all wet and muddy!"

Reluctantly, Brian did as he was bid but decided to kick a few pinecones instead. They continued walking, enveloped by the smell of the leaf mold from the rain-soaked earth. Under the giant pine trees and through an arbor of roses they came across what appeared to be a private garden, a sanctuary from the rest of the grounds, and in a corner was an old stone seat. They sat down and Janey said.

"Ma, will da get better?"

Not wanting to look her daughter in the eye Martha replied.

"We hope so, darling. But it will probably take a while"

Brian, his legs dangling from the seat said.

"How long ma?"

"I don't know pet. We will just have to wait and see. What about we say a little prayer for da while we are sitting here?"

As a nurse hurried by, she glimpsed through the arbor a woman, handkerchief to her eyes, and two children, with heads bowed and hands joined as though in prayer.

They had just arrived home when the telephone rang. Janey went to answer it.

"Hello," said her nanna.

"Hello, nan."

"Oh, Janey darling, how are you?"

"Well, thanks, nan. We have just got home from seeing da."

"Oh, have you. And how is he?"

"He doesn't look very well and finds it hard to talk. I wish he would get better," said Janey who noticed her mother coming into the hall.

"Oh well, I'm sure he will improve in time pet. He is in the best place and will be well looked after. Anyway, it won't be long until your holidays are here, and you and Brian can come to stay," said Nora.

"Yes, nan. I'm looking forward to that. How are the animals?"

"Oh, they're all good and as greedy as ever especially that Harold. He certainly eats like a pig!"

That remark put a smile on Janey's face which Martha was glad to see as lately there did not seem to be much to smile about.

Brian came barging in.

"Want to talk to nanna," he cried pulling the telephone out of his sister's hand.

"Wait a minute, Brian. Wait your turn," said Janey.

"Yes, pet wait until Janey finishes her conversation and then you can talk, and then it's my turn," said Martha.

Janey asked her nan if she was painting any more pictures then finishing her conversation, handed the telephone to her brother who now had sticky fingers as he had been helping himself to some jam he had found in the kitchen.

"Hello, nan. We saw our da today in the hospital, but it was cold 'cause the window was open and on the train, there was a man who had a cat in a basket but I couldn't pat him," said Brian nearly tripping over his words in his haste to tell his nanna all the news.

"Well, well, fancy that!" exclaimed Nora.

"Have you been a good boy at school?"

"Yes, nan."

"Nan?"

"Yes, darling".

"Can we stay at your house in the holidays?"

"Yes of course. I was just saying to Janey how it won't be long until your holidays."

Brian turned to his mother and told her that nan said they could stay at her place.

Martha smiled and said she needed to talk to nan now so Brian, happy that he would be soon going to his nan's, gave the telephone to his mother and scuttled off to his room to play with his train.

Janey had gone to the kitchen to make herself a fish-paste sandwich.

Martha took the telephone and settled herself on the chair then commenced to tell her mother about their day. She told her how worried she was about Tom, how he had a terrible pallor, how he seemed so thin and how he was so quiet, and that he was scheduled to have an operation on Wednesday. Nora listened to her daughter and tried to reassure her that all would be well in the end and just to take one day at a time.

They discussed the arrangements for the upcoming holidays which were only a few weeks away and decided that, depending on Tom's condition, Martha would accompany the children on the train.

Martha, a bit more reassured having spoken to her mother went to see about making the family some tea as it was now well past their mealtime.

Chapter Eight

It was Thursday, the day after Tom's operation and to Martha's relief, she had been informed that everything had gone well. She was on her way to the sanitarium having enlisted the help of her good neighbour in the event of her late arrival home.

In a white coat with a stethoscope poised over Tom's chest stood a doctor who turned around when Martha entered the room. He introduced himself as Doctor Atkins and then continued to apprise Martha of Tom's present condition. He explained that after an artificial pneumothorax the patient is required to lie flat for three days and refrain from reading. This allows for the other lung and heart to readjust. Then a few days later a refill is performed with the hope that a good general collapse would be seen on an x-ray.

Martha asked him what happens if there is no collapse and he said they would probably have to do the procedure again but would cross that bridge when they came to it. He then bustled off to his next patient leaving them alone again.

Martha sat on the chair and putting her bag on the floor, took Tom's hand and asked him how he was feeling. He said that his chest was sore, but he had been eating some of the food he was brought. He told her that they haven't been bringing any teaspoons with the tea and cocoa and you have to use the end of the knife to stir it. There is no separate bread and butter knife and everything is marked with the patient's number. He told her that everyone is classified as "on" something. If you had to use the basin you were "on basins" or "otw" meant out to wash. He said he was "on absolute" as he was entirely in bed. Martha thought the place was sounding more like a boarding school than a hospital but as long as it resulted in Tom's recovery that was all that mattered.

Martha told him that the children were looking forward to going to Cornwall for the holidays which were in a few weeks. She told him she had her suspicions that Mike's marriage was in trouble as he had volunteered to read to Helen's mum after work. Tom commented that was probably the reason why June said she was working after hours at Bletchley Park when she was probably with her lover. After a few more things were discussed, the visiting period had ended, and it was time for Martha to depart.

Kissing her husband and telling him she would try to see him soon; she left the room for the ancient lift to transport her to the foyer. After waiting for what seemed ages, it finally arrived, and she stepped inside and stood next to a doctor carrying a sheaf of papers. As the door clanged shut the lift gave a violent lurch and the papers fell from his hands.

"Oh damn," he cried as he stooped down to retrieve them.

"Let me help you," said Martha as she started scrabbling around the floor.

"Thank you, but it's no bother," he said grabbing some more as the lift descended slowly on its way.

Martha continued to help him and by the time they arrived at the foyer, all the papers had been collected.

"I say, thanks ever so much," he said. "This lift leaves a lot to be desired. I don't know how many times I have reported it to the board. They always say there are more things around here to spend money on and it is not on their priority list."

Martha replied, "Yes, I always enter the wretched thing with some trepidation. You never know if it's going to work or in which direction it will go."

"That's right. My thoughts exactly. I am doctor Young by the way," he said as he extended his free hand for Martha to shake.

"Pleased to meet you, doctor. I am Mrs. Johnson," Martha said shaking his hand.

"Oh, you must be Tom's wife in room 16?"

"Yes, that is my husband. Have you been treating him?"

"Only a couple of times. I usually have the night shift. He was due to have an artificial pneumothorax I believe."

"Yes, he had it yesterday. He said his chest was sore and he has to lie flat for a few days."

A porter staggered by carrying two cumbersome suitcases.

"Yes, that is the procedure. It gives the other lung and the heart time to readjust."

"That is what the other doctor told me," she said looking at her watch mindful of the time.

"By the way," she added, "I was wondering doctor if you are Edward. You see, I think I met your aunt the other day on the train. She told me that her nephew, Edward Young, was working at this sanitarium and might be treating my husband."

"What a coincidence!" he exclaimed. "Yes, I am Edward. I hope Aunt Joan had nice things to say about me!"

"Well, she didn't say much except you were in a clearing station in France. She seemed a very nice lady and cheered me up a bit."

"Yes, she is a good old stick," he noticed Martha again looking at her watch and said.

"I better let you go. Suppose you have a train to catch."

"Yes, as a matter of fact, I do. I live quite a way from here and I can't be late as I have two children at home although my kind neighbour is helping me out, thank goodness!"

"Well, have a safe journey home, Martha. The next time I look in on Tom, I will tell him I met you."

"Yes, do that, and thank you for looking after him. He's been through a lot and I'm so worried about him," she said tears threatening to spill from her eyes.

She hurried outside to a waiting taxi that drove her to the station where the train was waiting belching smoke into the air. To the sound of the whistle, Martha stepped aboard for another return journey to Uxbridge Road.

Thankfully the compartment was empty, so she was left alone to ponder the events of the day. Looking through the window her mind was filled with thoughts of her poor Tom having to lie flat in bed for days and having undergone an operation with no certainty of a good outcome. She thought of that doctor and could not believe she had run into him like that. What a small world it was! He seemed very nice, and she was a bit more reassured that Tom would be well looked after by him whenever he was rostered on a shift.

The day was quickly drawing to a close when Martha arrived at the station, so she hurriedly made her way home stopping at the grocer's for some eggs to make an omelette. As she passed the pub, she caught a glimpse of Mike's wife Jean who was snuggled in a corner with a man who was definitely not her husband! Tom must have been right, Martha thought. That must be the fellow she tossed Mike over for. She also thought it was strange that she would be required to work overtime now that the war had ended. Poor Mike, having done his duty for his country and losing his arm, now he was losing his wife as well. Life can be hard she thought. Everyone has some burden to bear. You never know what worries a person has. They might look cheerful on the outside, but inside their hearts could be breaking.

As she waited in the queue at the grocer's she thought of her dear Helen.

What a good kind friend she had been to Martha in her time of need. At the time, it seemed the only way, as she had been duped into thinking that the father would leave his wife and marry her. Oh, what a fool she had been! There was no way she could have looked after a baby, and she would have been a social outcast. There wasn't a day when she didn't think about the baby she had given up. Dear Helen, was the only person who knew what had happened as she could never tell her mother or Tom of the terrible things she had done. Helen had supported her above the call of duty, and she pledged that she would ring her friend tomorrow.

Arriving home, she was greeted by her two darling children and Ethel who was in a hurry to leave as it was her night to play bingo at the local hall.

"Thanks for minding them Ethel," she called after her. "And hope you win at bingo."

"Ta ra ducks. I hope I win and all. I could do with a few more pounds and no mistake!" shouted Ethel closing the door behind her.

Martha took off her coat and after hanging it on the rack went into the kitchen to make the tea.

The children came in and Janey asked.

"Ma, how was da today?"

"Oh, he was alright, only he has to lie flat in bed for a few days. He sends you and Brian a big hug each," Martha said as she broke the eggs into the bowl and commenced beating them with a fork.

Brian asked.

"What's for tea?"

Martha lit the stove.

"I'm making us an omelette. How was school today?"

"It was alright."

"I hope you ate your sandwiches."

"I only ate one and I swapped the other one with Herbie. I don't like fish paste. Herbie had jam sandwiches. I like those best."

"You can't have sweet things all the time pet. It's not good for you."

Martha pushed the egg around the pan and when it was cooked, she spooned their portions onto the plates and then boiled the kettle.

Janey put the bread and butter on the table, and they sat down to eat.

"I have such a lot of homework," said Janey as she buttered her bread.

"Do you darling?" asked Martha. "Well, as soon as you finish your tea you had better make a start."

"Oh, I have already. I did some before you came home."

Martha took a mouthful of tea "That's good then. Anyway, it won't be long until the holidays and you can have a break from homework."

"How many sleep days is it until the holidays ma?" asked Brian licking up the remains of the egg.

"It's about twenty-one Brian and stop licking the plate. It's not good manners," admonished his mother.

"You sound like grandma," said Brian.

That remark reminded Martha that she had not heard a word from the woman ever since that Sunday when they went to lunch. She was probably peeved with them after they had asked her for a loan of the money. She mentally added her to the list of people to be contacted tomorrow.

Chapter Nine

The children having left for school Martha thought she would try to ring Tom's mother before she pegged out the washing.

She dialled the number and Phyllis the maid's nasally voice answered.

"Johnson residence."

"Hello, it's Martha Johnson, Tom's wife. May I speak to Sylvia please?"

"She's not here," she replied.

"Oh, when will she be returning?"

"Don't know. She's in the hospital."

Martha looked concerned "In the hospital?" she queried "What's wrong with her?"

"She came a cropper and broke her hip."

"When did that happen?" asked Martha becoming more perplexed.

"Can't remember," said Phyllis. "Think it was a couple of weeks ago."

"Oh, I see. Well, do you know at which hospital she is?"

"Wait there. I wrote it down somewhere."

She left Martha hanging on for ages while she went off to try and find where she had written the address.

Finally, she came back on the line.

"Are you there?" she questioned.

"Yes, of course, I'm still here," said Martha with impatience growing, thinking of the washing to be pegged and other chores she could be doing instead of waiting around for the ditzy maid to get organised.

"She's in the Lister hospital," she explained.

"Is that in Belgravia?" asked Martha now fed up with her one-sentence replies.

"On what street is it located?"

Phyllis replied, "Don't know."

"Oh, then I shall have to look it up in the telephone book, thank you," putting the phone down in exasperation she located the book and flicking through eventually found the address which was Chelsea Bridge Road, and the telephone number.

She dialled and was put through to the ward in which Sylvia was confined and eventually was told that her mother-in-law had indeed broken her hip and was expected to remain in hospital for another six weeks. Thereafter to be admitted to a convalescent hospital for another two months or so depending on her ability to walk. She was told that the patient was as well as to be expected and could receive visitors.

Martha was quite taken aback by all these developments. She must try to visit her even though they didn't get on, but she was Tom's mother after all and it was the charitable thing to do.

She finished sorting the washing and after making herself a strong cup of tea rang the sanitarium to check on Tom's condition. She was informed that he was on two pillows today and he was also as well as could be expected. The standard hospital phrase thought Martha. All the patients were as well as could be expected! But at least Tom's condition had not changed so that was a bonus.

Putting on her coat and applying some lipstick she took her bag and headed off for the next bus which would transport her to Chelsea Bridge Road.

She arrived at the hospital after an arduous trip on the bus. There was a lot of traffic and roadworks on the south Ealing Road did nothing to hasten the journey. After locating the correct ward and room Martha found her mother-in-law sitting up in bed deep in conversation with a stylish-looking woman. She was adorned with pearls and what looked like a mink fur around her bony shoulders and there was a plethora of Harrods bags at her feet.

"Ah, Martha," exclaimed her mother-in-law.

"Hello Sylvia," said Martha approaching the bed "How are you? I didn't know you had an accident."

"Yes, I did as a matter of fact. Slipped on the tiles," she replied.

She looked over at the stylish personage. "Edwina, this is my daughter-in-law, Martha."

"How do you do?" she said looking Martha up and down.

Martha was conscious of her somewhat dowdy appearance, and she could sense her face flushing.

"Well, sit down," Sylvia instructed.

Martha sat.

Popping a grape into her mouth she asked.

"So how is Thomas? Is he in the sanitarium?"

Martha replied.

"Yes, Sylvia he is, and he is not very well. He had to have an artificial pneumothorax the other day and is trying to recover."

"Oh, is that so?"

She turned to Edwina and explained that Tom had been a prisoner of war and now was suffering from TB. She told her friend of her feelings about the war and that she had been totally against her son enlisting in the first place.

Her friend nodded as if in agreement.

"What is your husband's prognosis?" she asked looking down her nose at Martha.

"Well, at the moment we are just taking things one day at a time I'm afraid. It will take a while before he is fully recovered," Martha said wishing that the woman would leave soon as she was feeling rather uncomfortable. It was bad enough having to weather Sylvia's attitude let alone her snooty friend.

Then a nurse bustled in to enquire if the patient required anything.

Sylvia said.

"Yes, could you ask the maid if she would remember to change the water in the vases? I can't abide stale water."

"Very well, Mrs. Johnson I will notify one of the nurses," said the nurse and scuttled out the door before any more orders were made.

"It's the same everywhere," piped up madam stylish. "You cannot get the help to do what they ought. Even here in the hospital!"

"That's quite right Edwina," interjected Sylvia popping another grape and not offering any to Martha.

"My maid Phyllis leaves a lot to be desired. Why I remember in the days before the war the servants knew their places and their duties without one having to tell them!"

Edwina added.

"Absolutely, Sylvia. It's a different world now. The help think they are our equals!"

And so, they continued to swap opinions about the class system and their servants until Edwina looked at her diamond-encrusted watch.

"Oh, is that the time? Well, I'm afraid I have to love you and leave you, Sylvia. I have a facial booked at Valois then we are entertaining the Ridsdales."

She blew a kiss at the patient and gathered up her bags.

"Goodbye," she said and swanned off past Martha, Chanel no 5 drifting in her wake.

Thank goodness she has gone, thought Martha, and it won't be long until I take my leave. Her mother-in-law obviously had no interest in anyone but herself.

"Well, that was excellent of dear Edwina to pop in albeit a flying visit" she twittered "I suppose you must go soon too."

"Yes, Sylvia I have to catch the bus. It took a while to get here. There were roadworks and quite a lot of traffic."

"Oh, public transport!" she exclaimed "Sitting with all those strange people. One would never know what germs one would catch!"

Sighing, Martha replied.

"Well, for some of us there is no alternative, I'm afraid. Now I was told you will have to go to a convalescent home when you are discharged from here. Is that right?" asked Martha.

Looking rather crestfallen she replied.

"Yes, apparently. I'm not fond of the idea. Those places are full of old people. I really would prefer to be in my own home being looked after by someone I know. You wouldn't consider it would you?"

Martha looked concerned, "Consider what Sylvia?"

"Oh, you know looking after me, and so on. Phyllis would be there to do the rough work."

Martha was taken aback by this idea of her mother-in-law.

"You mean be your paid nursemaid, Sylvia?"

"Yes, that is what I mean. With Thomas in that place for months and the children at school, it would be ideal, and you would have a little income" she said straightening the sheet.

"Oh, well I could do with some extra money now you mention it. But I have to give it some thought. How much were you thinking of offering me?"

"I haven't thought about the amount yet. When you have decided to let me know and we will come to some arrangement."

"Oh, alright I will let you know when I have given it some thought" replied Martha looking at her watch and deciding to leave if she was to catch the next bus.

"I must go now, Sylvia. I will be in touch. Take care of yourself" Martha said going over and patted her hand as that was about all she could demonstrate in the way of affection towards her.

"Goodbye," said Sylvia, "and let me know what you decide as there will have to be arrangements made regarding the convalescent home."

The cheek of the woman Martha thought to herself as she sat on the bus. Asking me to be her nursemaid! She knew she could do with some money but looking after her? It was all a bit much to take in. I will ring mum and Helen and see what they think she thought as the bus swerved to avoid hitting a pedestrian nearly sending Martha flying off the seat.

At last, she came to her stop and decided to call at the shops as she had run out of milk and potatoes and needed to buy some mince as she was making a cottage pie tonight. As she entered the butcher shop, she thought she recognised the lady to whom she was talking on the train- the doctor's aunt, Joan.

"Oh hello," Martha said, "I thought I recognised you."

"Oh, it's Martha, isn't it? What a coincidence bumping into you?" exclaimed Joan putting her parcel of meat in her basket.

"Yes, it is. How have you been?" replied Martha making her way to the counter "A pound of mince please," she told the butcher after he had asked her what she wanted.

"Oh, I'm well thanks," said Joan.

Martha paid for her mince and the two of them left the shop.

"If you're not in a hurry, do you want to have a cup of tea and maybe some cake?" asked Joan.

"Oh, that sounds lovely. I certainly could do with a cuppa. Let's go into Mollie's."

They walked on with their baskets and settled themselves down in a window seat in the tea shop.

"We'll have two teas and two slices of that lovely cake you have on the counter," Joan told the waitress as she came to take the order.

Joan said.

"Well, Martha. How is your husband progressing at the sanitarium?"

"He had to have an operation, a pneumothorax. I do hope it will be successful otherwise he might have to have another. I'm so worried about him. He has a terrible pallor and is so thin" Martha told her companion tears beginning to form.

Seeing her distress, Joan patted her hand "Now, now, don't worry so much dear" she said "I'm sure he will recover in time. I don't suppose he has run into Edward?"

The waitress came with their order and Martha commenced pouring their tea.

"As a matter of fact, you wouldn't believe it, but I actually met your nephew in the lift, I helped him pick up some papers he had dropped!"

"No, you never did. What a coincidence!" said Joan nibbling some of her cake.

"Yes, wasn't it? He seemed very nice and said he hoped you were saying good things about him."

"That would be just like him. He has a fine sense of humour. It has put him in good stead to weather what life has thrown at him."

Martha sipped her tea.

"Oh, what happened?" she queried.

Joan wiped her mouth with the napkin and leaned toward Martha.

"His wife was pregnant with their first child when she contracted TB and died while giving birth."

"Oh, that's terrible," cried Martha putting down her cup.

"Yes, it was. Apparently, Nicky had rheumatic fever as a child and it weakened her heart, so with the combination of that and tuberculosis she didn't have much of a chance."

"Oh, the poor thing and poor Edward. That's so sad. I'm sorry to hear that, Joan."

"Now, Martha, you shouldn't let what I said worry you more about Tom. As I said, Nicky did not have a strong constitution."

Martha nodded and they continued with their afternoon tea.

"That is one of the reasons Edward is working in the sanitarium trying to help the people with this wretched disease," Joan added.

"That's very commendable of him," said Martha.

They paid the bill and walked outside.

"That was nice to catch up," said Joan.

"Yes, it was, very nice. If you feel like meeting again give me a ring" said Martha as she pulled out a piece of paper and commenced writing her number on it.

"Thanks, Martha, I will do that. If I can have the pencil, I will write my number down as well."

They exchanged numbers and went their separate ways. Martha to prepare the cottage pie and Joan to board her bus.

Chapter Ten

Nora was exasperated with her latest work. She couldn't get it to look right. The new paint she had ordered was not as good as the usual one. She would just have to send it back to the shop. She screwed on the lid and thought a nice cup of tea would calm her down. Going to the Aga she put the kettle onto boil and heard the telephone ringing.

"Hello," she answered.

"Hello, mum," said Martha. "How are you?"

Nora settled herself down in the chair for a welcome conversation with her daughter.

"I'm good thanks darling, except for some exasperation with the new paint I ordered."

"Oh, sorry to hear that mum. Can you send it back?"

"Yes, that's what I'll have to do. Send it back and tell them to give me the old tried and true. I shouldn't have listened to that salesman. He could sell snow to Eskimos!"

Nora settled further into the chair and was glad she had purchased it all those years ago. It was so comfortable she felt she could easily sleep in it.

"Mum," said Martha. "Sylvia broke her hip. I only found out when I rang her house, and that maid Phyllis told me she was in the hospital."

"Oh, is that so?" You would think she would have let you know," Nora said. "She could have told the maid to ring you."

"Yes, that's what I thought. Anyway, I went to see her yesterday. She is in the Lister Hospital. There was one of her snooty friends visiting when I arrived. I was glad when she left. But listen to this, the upshot was that when she is discharged, she is supposed to be admitted to a convalescent home which she detests," Martha sneezed.

"Go on," encouraged Nora.

"Well, she then proceeded to ask me if I would go over and be her nursemaid and help her out during the hours the children are at school, and she would pay me like a regular job. What do you think of that?"

Nora ran her fingers through her hair.

"I don't know what to say to that!" she said.

"No, it certainly took me aback. But the thing is mum, I need to have an income with Tom the way he is. I don't think he will ever be able to work again, and the thought crossed my mind that I should have some sort of part-time job."

"Yes, but Martha," said Nora. "Looking after that woman? She would drive you mad."

"I know mum. She is difficult but I thought I might give it a go and if it doesn't work out I can always leave and try to find something else."

"Well, it's your decision darling," said Nora. "But remember what I said about the loan. I don't expect you to pay me back."

"I know mum and thank you for that, but I really feel I need to have some extra money. It is an extra concern on top of the worry about Tom."

"Alright, Martha, dear I will support you in whatever you decide but if it all becomes too much just look for something else."

"I will mum, and thanks for your advice and support. The children are looking forward to their visit."

"Yes, it's not long now. Give the pets hugs and kisses and tell them nan can't wait to see them."

"I will mum. Take care of yourself, talk to you soon."

After speaking to her mother Martha felt more reassured about her decision to look after her mother-in-law. She thought she would now talk to Helen to elicit her opinion although she knew what her response was going to be!

"What? Look after that old biddy? Martha, you must be joking!" Helen spluttered through the telephone.

"I know she is difficult Helen, but I thought I can at least try it out. I can always throw in the towel if she becomes too obstreperous."

"Well, it's your funeral as they say!" said her friend.

"Thanks, you are a tonic. Anyway, how is everything? How's Val and did Mike ever come over and read to her?"

"Oh, the questions," she said.

"Mum is about the same but when Mike comes over, she really perks up."

"So, he has been over then?"

"Oh yes, he comes over after work and lately has been staying for tea."

Martha's ears pricked up.

"Oh, has he? Has he said anything to you about his marriage?"

"Yes, he told me that his wife has left him and that he had had suspicions for a while that she has been seeing someone else," Helen said.

"Yes, I also had my suspicions but didn't want to make them known. I used to think it was strange that his wife would still be required to work after hours at that Bletchley Park now that the war has ended. I couldn't imagine what she would be doing there."

Martha heard the door open, and Brian barged in with his school satchel. Janey had gone to her friend's house.

"Just a minute Helen, Brian has come home."

She told him to scoot off and have a biscuit while she was talking to her friend.

"Sorry about that Helen, now what was I saying?"

"You were saying about Mike's wife's story about working at Bletchley."

"Oh, that's right, and also when I was coming home from seeing Tom a while back, I happened to catch a glimpse of her in the pub with her fancy man," said Martha.

"Oh, really?" said Helen surprised.

She continued, "Mike's such a nice man, Marth. He doesn't deserve to be treated like that"

"No, he doesn't," agreed Martha. "I'm glad he is reading to Val. It must give her something to look forward to."

"Yes, it certainly does. Well, I had better go and see if mum needs anything before, I make a start on the tea."

"Oh, with all the talk about the curmudgeon," she added. "I haven't asked you about Tom."

"He had to have an operation," replied Martha. "An artificial pneumothorax it's called. He's recovering from that at the moment. He had to lie flat on the bed for a couple of days and increase the number of pillows thereafter."

"Yes, I've heard about that operation. Hopefully, that will do the trick."

"Oh, I do hope so Helen. I'm so worried about him. He is so thin, and he has lost the zest for life that he used to have."

"Well, considering what he has been through it's no wonder."

"That's right. Well, I had better go and see what Brian is up to. He has probably gone through the whole tin of biscuits by now."

"I hope not for your sake, Marth. Thanks for ringing and give my love to Tom and the children."

"I will. Bye Helen, love to Val."

Martha hung up the telephone and went to find Brian who was nowhere to be seen. She went up to his room and found him in the corner playing with his soldiers, a collection of biscuits strewn around the floor.

Chapter Eleven

The weeks had passed, school holidays had arrived, and Martha and the children were at Paddington station ready to board the train which would transport them to nanna's house in Cornwall. Martha had decided to accompany them and stay for the weekend as she felt she needed a break, and also to see her mother. She had notified the sanitarium she would be away and left her mother's number in case they had to contact her. She prayed that there would not be any bad news, and Tom would remain stable.

To the sound of the guard's whistle, they had settled themselves into a compartment after stowing their luggage in the racks with the help of a kind old gentleman who had witnessed Martha's struggle.

The outskirts of London soon gave way to the green fields of the countryside with Brian exclaiming how many sheep and tractors he could see. He had been beside himself with excitement since he woke before dawn impatient to leave. Now, here he was on his way to nanna's for two weeks of carefree holiday. He thought about the times he had stayed with his mother and sister and of nanna's animals which he loved, especially Harold whose back he loved to scratch, as his snout snuffled in the dirt, and Lucy the goat who liked to be chased.

He loved to look for the eggs the chooks had laid and, finding some, proudly carried them into nanna for her to make a delicious breakfast or, even better, beat them for a cake. He wished his da was coming with them instead of being in that place which let in the cold all day. He found it hard to understand that leaving the windows open when it was cold would make his da better as windows were usually firmly shut to keep the cold out. Life was certainly hard to understand at times he thought as another black sheep came into view.

Martha looked over at her daughter. She was still ensconced in her book. She certainly likes reading Martha thought. Since Tom had come home, she noticed Janey seemed quiet and withdrawn and not like the happy little girl she used to be chattering away about all and sundry. I suppose it's her age, Martha thought. She was twelve, on the cusp of womanhood, with all that entailed. I will have to ensure she does not mix with anyone unsuitable and not be led astray. Her friend Maisie was a nice little thing, well brought up by caring parents however, that other girl in her class who had tried to befriend Janey left a lot to be desired She was a precocious little miss, was twelve going on twenty! Martha had heard that the house in which she lived with her mother had men going in and out at all hours of the day and night: the collection of empty bottles of ale and spirits doing nothing to enhance the respectability of the place.

Martha pondered about her abilities of being a good mother, raising her children to grow up fine upstanding citizens. It was certainly not an easy job raising children. She thought about how she had been raised by her mother and still, she had managed to fall by the wayside. Please god, don't let Janey get entangled with some fellow and end up pregnant and abandoned as she had done!

Resting her cheek on the window as the train took them further on to Cornwall Martha was transported back to the time she had spent with the sadistic nuns and all the unmarried mothers in that hell hole of a convent in Croydon.

From the first time she entered that pristine foyer which she saw was being kept that way by two heavily pregnant girls down on their knees, rags, and brushes in hand scrubbing and polishing, she knew that her life would be descending into misery.

The dour-faced nun having assessed Martha and taken down all relevant details summoned one of the girls who had been cleaning the floor. She was taken to the dormitory where she would sleep with other girls until she gave birth to her child. Iron beds devoid of curtains with not a modicum of privacy offered stood on a scuffed lino floor in the cold featureless room. A picture of the Sacred Heart looked down from the wall onto all the poor sinners beneath.

Every morning at 4:30 am one of the girls would ring a bell and everyone would stagger out of bed to line up at the sinks in the freezing bathroom to have a quick wash before walking single file to the chapel. There they would stand and kneel while the priest conducted a mass and admonished them for falling from grace and giving themselves up to the temptations of the flesh.

After this they would go to something passing for breakfast: a bowl of glutinous porridge and a cup of stewed tea all consumed in complete silence as was the rule at mealtimes.

Then it was the laundry where in the hot, steamy confines, the clothing of the nuns and others of the outside community was boiled, starched, mangled, and ironed. Woe betides anyone who happened to faint as was frequently the case as she would be put into the "black hole" under the stairs to contemplate her misdemeanours.

Laundry duty done, there was a respite as they could at least sit down and have dinner, but this was as unappetising as the breakfast. Ladled onto the grey cracked plates used by the inmates before them, the tough mutton and over-cooked cabbage did nothing to assuage their hunger.

Then, plates scraped into the slop pails, the unfortunate girl who was rostered on for washing up would, to the shrieks of the supervising nun, have her head pushed into the scummy water as a lesson to do better.

There was an hour after lunch when there was a relaxation period but, even then, if a nun took a dislike to someone she could be dragged by her hair off a chair or slapped around the head for no better reason than nodding off while reading a book.

The drab grey building surrounded by a barbed wire fence made the place feel like a jail. Martha found herself wishing for the time when she would give birth and re-enter the freedom of the outside world which she had more or less taken for granted up until now.

So the months wore on, and the only day Martha looked forward to was Sunday, as that was the day everyone was allowed visitors, and to leave the premises for an hour. Helen used to see Martha on Sundays and they would head for the nearest park. Sitting on a blanket on the grass if the weather was fine, Martha would pour out her troubles to her friend. Helen would always reassure her that all the misery would soon pass, and she would be out of the place ready to start a new chapter of her life.

On these weekly visits, Martha would give her friend a letter to post to her mother. In the letter Martha would write about the great time she was having at the hostel, and how she was making good progress with shorthand and typing. She hated to tell her mother lies but she did not have any other choice. Helen gladly posted her letters as the only time Martha was permitted to venture outside was when a doctor had to be visited for a check-up. Accompanied by another girl, they would walk to the appointment sporting cheap rings on their wedding fingers for respectability.

Soon it was Martha's time, and as rain lashed the building and the wind penetrated every crack, Martha was overtaken by the pains of labour. After eight hours of excruciating agony relieved only marginally by a tiny amount of gas, she finally gave birth to a baby boy. He was whisked away immediately to the nursery where he would stay until his adoptive parents came to claim him.

After being stitched with no anaesthetic to blunt the pain, Martha was left bereft and abandoned on the bed. After a while, Sister Mathilda appeared carrying some bandages and, with her breasts bound, Martha was sent back to the after-care dormitory in which lay other grieving mothers who had recently given birth. There they swapped stories of their ordeals, while others in floods of tears rocked on their beds in grief pining for the babies they had given away to strangers.

Martha signed the papers on a Tuesday, her signature blotted by tears that fell onto the page. She tried to think it was all for the best, her baby would be given a better life than she could have given it. Now she could resume her life, and hopefully, meet someone and marry and have more babies to love and nurture. However, as she organised her belongings in the flat, she shared with Helen, she thought she would never forget the baby she had surrendered and that terrible place of her confinement.

Martha was brought out of her reverie by the guard announcing that they had one stop to go. Alerting Brian whose interest was still in counting the sheep, she gathered together her basket and bag and Janey helped her pull the suitcase off the rack.

In a cloud of steam, the train drew into the station and disgorged its passengers to be met by a welcoming throng. Suddenly there appeared an overweight lady in a yellow floral dress and a straw sun hat waving her arms.

"Nanna!" cried Brian running over to her followed closely by his sister and Martha.

"Hello, pets. Did you have a good journey?" Nanna said enveloping them all in a big bear hug.

Nora helped Martha with the suitcase and bags and the foursome walked a short distance to where the little Austin was parked and, squeezing in, they set off for Polperro.

"Now, how about a nice piece of cake and a cup of tea?" Nora asked after Martha had sorted out an argument between Brian and Janey about in which bed they would sleep. Janey indignant that she always likes to be near the window and Brian wanting the same. Finally, it was decided that they would take turns. One week on and one week off.

"Oh, mum," said Martha as she settled herself on the chair in the kitchen "I could murder a cup of tea right now."

Brian came in and sat down next to his mother.

"I'm sure you don't want some cake do you Brian?" ribbed Nora as she sliced the cake into pieces.

"Nan," cried Brian. "I want some cake!"

"Oh, I thought you might have stopped liking cake, Brian. But I'm glad you haven't because I made this, especially for you and Janey" said Nora bringing over the plates.

Martha went to the Aga and poured the boiled water into the teapot and put it on the table.

"I can't believe you've still got this pot mum" commented Martha as she placed it on the table "It must be so old now. You've had it for ages."

"Yes, it's a wonder I haven't broken it by now with all the use it's had. I haven't seen another one like it in any of the shops."

Janey came in and sat down

"Well," said Nora settling herself in her chair "Here we are again, all together."

They commenced eating and Nora asked the children how they were progressing at school but avoided mentioning anything about their father as that subject would be broached when the children were not around.

Brian finished his cake and asked his nanna if he could go outside to see the animals, especially Harold who he was dying to see. Janey decided that she would go too and after they had gone Nora asked Martha all about Tom.

She told her how worried she was about him in that cold draughty place. How terrible he always looked and that his life's spark seemed to be slowly extinguishing before her eyes. She told her how she had met on the train the aunt of the doctor at the sanitarium and of meeting him in the lift, and that she had caught up with his aunt at a tea shop not far from Uxbridge Road.

Nora listened to her daughter and tried to console her as best she could when she noticed tears welling up in Martha's eyes just as the children trooped in, Brian managing to have his pants covered in mud.

"Oh, Brian, look at the state of your pants," cried Martha in exasperation. "Have you been rolling around in the mud with Harold?"

"But mum, I didn't mean to. Harold knocked me over!"

"I don't know Brian, what I'm to do with you," said Martha hauling him over to the sink in a vain attempt to clean off some of the mud.

Meanwhile, Nora took her granddaughter into her little studio to have a look at the painting which was still in progress. Janey was filled with wonder as she admired her nanna's work.

"Would you like to try and paint something Janey?" asked Nora. "Your mother was telling me you like to draw at school."

"Oh, yes I quite like to draw Nan, but I don't think I would ever be able to paint like you."

"Well, I didn't paint like that either when I was your age. It takes lots of practice, pet. But if you don't give it a go you may never know if you have the talent. Nothing ventured, nothing gained is my motto," said Nora setting up some paper on an easel and rummaging around for a suitable brush.

She sat Janey down and after showing her how to mix the various colours guided her through a few basic strokes. With her tongue licking her bottom lip in concentration Janey surprised herself when a picture started to emerge on the paper.

"That's great love," exclaimed Nora. "Now I think if we just put a little bit more red here" and Janey did as her nanna instructed.

"Well, I think you have made an excellent start young lady and you never know by the end of the holidays you might be good enough to enrol in an art class after school"

"Oh Nan, ma wouldn't be able to afford that," Janey said putting her brush into the jar of turpentine as Nora had instructed.

"Well, we'll see what can be done. Where there's a will there's a way as the saying goes," said Nora ruffling Janey's hair.

And she added, "There might be a class run by the council for talented children like you. I'll ask your mother to make some enquiries. Anyway, that's enough for now. It's time for tea shortly and there are the beans to top and tail, and the potatoes to peel. How about we go and round up Brian and your mother?"

They found Martha lying on the bed her arm stretched out in a pose of sleep snoring quietly. Nora pulled the eiderdown over her daughter and they tiptoed out of the room. Brian was nowhere to be seen.

"Now where's that scallywag brother of yours got to I wonder?" asked Nora as she went from room to room calling his name but none of the rooms contained Brian.

"He's probably outside again nan, playing with Harold or Lucy," said Janey opening the back door.

"Yes, I'll bet that's where he is. Probably rolling around in the mud again, little devil!" said Nora.

They both went outside and up into the field where the animals usually roamed.

"Brian, Brian," they called. "Where are you?"

But there was no answer and no sign of Brian.

By now the last rays of the sun were disappearing over the horizon and Nora was starting to worry. Where could he have got to she asked herself? If I find him, I will box his ears!

Looking worried Janey said "Gosh Nan, where could he be? Ma will be so worried if he doesn't turn up soon."

Nora tried to be reassuring and told Janey, "Don't worry pet. I'm sure we will find him."

Martha's hair disheveled from sleep came running towards them.

"Mum, what's going on? I must have dozed off. Where's Brian?"

"Oh, Martha we don't know. Janey and I were in the studio and when we came out there was no sign of him. I'm sure he can't be far," said Nora trying to be calm.

"Brian where are you?" screamed Martha at the top of her voice.

"Mum, we have to call someone. Call the police. It's getting dark now."

Nora told Martha to stay with Janey and she would go down to the house and summon help

Martha watched her mother disappear in the descending gloom then, grabbing Janey her tearful face mixing with the brown strands of her daughter's hair she cried for her little boy lost.

Please God, she prayed, bring my baby back to me safe and sound. Don't let anything bad have happened to him. I don't care how much mud he manages to get on his clothes, or how many biscuits he eats, just as long as he is safe.

Janey sensing her mother's anguish also started to cry and through her sobs asked.

"Ma, will they find him?"

Before Martha had time to answer there was a rustle of leaves and Nora appeared accompanied by two policemen.

"Good evening," said the larger of the two "Now I believe we have a missing boy."

"Oh yes," Martha said trying to compose herself and knowing she must look a sight with her tear-stained face and messy hair

"We can't find him. We've been calling his name and tried to search for him but it's dark now. Oh please, can you find him?"

Opening a notebook, the policeman commenced jotting down some notes and asked Martha and Nora when was the last time they saw the youngster. Nora told him that they were all in the kitchen eating cake and then Nora and Janey went into the studio. Martha said that she last saw him in the kitchen and then she had gone to lie down on the bed and had drifted off to sleep.

"Well, I'm sure he can't have gone too far. I'll get my partner here to enlist the help of some of the locals and between us, we will be able to cover more ground."

The younger policeman torch on, disappeared into the darkness towards the village to rouse the locals to help in the search for little Brian.

"This fence seems to be broken," exclaimed policeman one as he shone his torch around the area alighting on the barbed wire fence. "Have you noticed any pets missing at all?"

Nora went over and suddenly realised that Lucy was not around.

"Oh, goodness," she cried. "Lucy!"

"What mum?" Martha asked, "Has Lucy gone too?"

"I can't hear her anywhere. She usually makes a racket at this time of night if anyone's around and with all the worry about Brian I hadn't taken any notice that she wasn't here," said Nora.

They all scrambled over to the fence which contained a gap wide enough to let a small goat and a small boy through just as the sounds of voices drifted towards them through the dew-filled night.

Lamps and torches in hand the villagers came tramping towards them all anxious to find the lost boy from Ealing.

"Now, ladies and gentlemen," announced policeman one. "It seems as if the boy may have gone off with the pet goat. I think we should concentrate our efforts down the track towards the cliff."

Addressing Martha, Nora, and Janey he said,

"It might be advisable if you three stay put here in case the boy shows up."

Immediately Martha yelled, "I want to go with the others. I can't just wait around here doing nothing"

Nora said it would be best if Martha went and she and Janey would stay.

Agreeing to that the policeman and Martha, beside herself with worry, squeezed through the opening of the fence and followed the searchers. Calling out Brian's name they shone their lights into bushes and behind rocks all to no avail. Martha's heart beating rapidly and her mind zeroing in on the worst possible scenario for her child she and the searchers pushed on towards the cliff.

Chapter Twelve

Tom, dirty, exhausted and down to his last cigarette looked from his dug-out at the bloodied beach which was covered by the body parts of his mates who had been killed in the last days in this hell hole of a place called Dunkerque. As another bomb exploded sending sand and shrapnel into the eyes and ears of the remaining British army, Tom's hopes of being rescued were fading by the minute.

He had lost sight of Mike a long time ago and did not know if he was still alive or was one of the poor souls rotting on the beach, to be swept away into the boiling ocean.

God, it was a bugger of a war! When he had enlisted with the other fellows all full of their duty to king and country and all impatient to give those Hun a good licking, he really never envisaged what had lay ahead of them. Coming from quite a privileged background with all the benefits that entailed, then to university, and into a sedentary role in the office, was miles away from the conditions in which he found himself now. The worsening noise of the guns and bombs assailed Tom's eardrums until he felt as though he was deaf.

Then the marching left right, left right, schnell, schnell! Germans prodded them with guns or slapped them around their heads if they did not move fast enough. They were the unfortunate ones who had missed out on being rescued by the flotilla of boats sent by Churchill and their final destination was Trier many miles further on.

With every painful step, he visualised his darling Martha keeping the home fires burning and rearing his daughter Janey and her baby brother Brian. Oh god, how he missed them. What he would not give to be in their cosy house at Uxbridge Road just living a normal family life, sitting in front of the fire, reading the newspaper. Even the smell of Brian's nappies soaking in the pail would have been balm to his senses.

His bleeding, blistered feet trudged on over the rough terrain, and many times he fell to the ground only to be kicked in the stomach, then helped up by one of his fitter comrades who was also kicked in the kidneys for his trouble.

Finally, the sorry bedraggled bunch arrived at their destination and were herded through the gate of a camp surrounded by barbed wire, watched over by machine gun-wielding guards. They were pushed into a building containing bunks with one blanket and no pillow and then were told to be outside in half an hour for rollcall, which was to be their daily pattern from 4:00 am no matter what the weather.

Their diet consisting of watery soup and bread did nothing to contribute to their health. Tom developed a persistent cough and bouts of severe diarrhea which, combined with his now infected feet, rendered him almost useless for much activity. He was unable to participate in the occasional cricket match bargained by the officers from the German command to try and lift the spirits of the men.

Then the transportation to that factory, where the rest of his days were spent with other sufferers assembling parts for the German war machine. The women, or what passed as women, gaunt, soulless eyes trying to concentrate on the task, brought in from Ravensbruck to swell the numbers of the slaves, keeling over from lack of food and unspeakable horrors foisted upon them in the camp.

Hobbling towards him one day, a new arrival, a blond polish gypsy whispering how she and others named "rabbits" had been guinea pigs for experimentation by a Doctor Rosenthal at the camp on the orders of Himmler. She tells him how her legs had been opened, how bacteria had been inserted with glass and bits of wood: how in agony her suppurating legs had leaked brown fluid in the bed, and bandages applied up to her groin. After removal, she and the others saw their wounds for the first time, the incisions on the tibias so deep they could see the bone. She tells of their raging thirst as they were denied any water, parched lips bleeding, and bedpans so full they could not be used. How the stench of rotting flesh permeated the room in which they were kept, turning the strongest stomach.

He listened in shock as she whispered that her friend had contracted tetanus from one such experiment dying in agony to the laughter of the sadistic nurses. Through clenched teeth because of a locked jaw, she had managed to ask about her two small children then, with a final terrible scream, her life had ended.

How there was a midwife who was methodically killing the newborn babies letting them die in their cots through lack of food or care and also of killing the patients by injections of phenol or petrol.

Every day they sat together Tom trying to lift her flagging spirits, sometimes giving her his meagre ration of bread which she devoured like an animal. On the final day before she was transported back to the camp, either to be exterminated elsewhere or to die there she whispered to him that if he survived, he must let the world know of the barbarism being conducted at Ravensbruck.

Through the fog of his delirium, Tom felt a wet compress on his forehead bringing him back to the surroundings of his room at Frimley, a doctor and a nurse hovering over his bed

"Well, old chap," he said, "You had us worried for a while."

Tom, thankful for not being back in that factory and still alive, albeit very ill, succumbed to the gentle ministrations of his carers.

Chapter Thirteen

It was the next day that they discovered Brian. Lying in a small bush protruding from the cliff, he had been saved from certain death on the rocks below where the unfortunate goat had met her fate.

From the hospital bed after regaining consciousness, Brian had explained how he had gone looking for Lucy and discovered that she had broken through the fence. He had spotted her and chased her along to the cliff edge where she had taken fright and jumped with Brian losing his footing and also falling over the edge.

Martha, Nora, and Janey having not had a wink of sleep had rushed to the cliff after the authorities alerted them to the discovery when the search had been resumed at first light. One of the rescuers was sent over the cliff by a rope and then he and Brian had been winched up to the relief and cheers of the assembled throng. Martha had rushed over followed quickly by Nora and Janey and, with tears of relief and joy, smothered him with kisses.

"Oh my baby!" she cried "You're safe, you're alive!"

Brian still dazed seemed unaware of the concern around him and then with Martha by his side he had been whisked away in an ambulance, siren blaring to the local hospital. Nora took Janey back to the cottage where, after strong cups of tea and toast they both took themselves to bed for a much-needed sleep.

Martha stayed by her son's bedside as he spent the day and night under observation. Martha was so pleased that her old Brian was back as he whined and whinged about the nurses' shining torches in his eyes at regular intervals.

"Mum," said Martha when they arrived back at the cottage after Brian was discharged from the hospital. "Do you think you can cope with the children for the holidays?"

Nora taking a batch of scones out of the Aga turned to her daughter.

"Of course, dear, why wouldn't I cope?"

"I just thought with all that's happened it might be too much worry."

"Nonsense," she replied opening the cupboard to locate the strawberry jam.

"Accidents will happen, and I don't expect anything like that to occur again. You just stop your worrying, go back home and enjoy a couple of weeks free from the children."

Martha said, "Alright mum, if, you're sure."

"Quite sure, now sit down and have some scones."

"Janey," she called. "Come and have a scone darling."

Martha put a scone and covering it with jam and cream took it to Brian who was sitting up in bed. Apart from a lump on his forehead which was turning a deep shade of purple, he seemed none the worse for wear. The scone was soon devoured with Brian demanding to have another soon after. Although he was initially upset about the demise of Lucy, he soon overcame it and bounced back to his usual cheerful self.

"It's good Brian has his normal appetite," Martha said to her mother as she came into the kitchen to collect another scone.

"Little devil," Nora said. "We don't have to worry about him. The day he refuses his nan's scones will be the time for concern."

Janey said licking her fingers of jam.

"Ma, will you be going home today or tomorrow?"

"Probably tomorrow darling. I think I would rather stay another night to see how Brian fares and then catch the 10.30 back."

"Ok" she replied.

"Are you going to try and paint some more in the holidays?" Martha asked, "Your first attempt looked rather promising."

"Yes, I think I might, I enjoyed it," said Janey adding, "Ma, nanna said that she thought I might be able to enrol in an art class after school."

Martha looked a bit taken aback, mentally calculating how much money that would cost and if they could afford such a luxury.

"Well, we'll see darling," she said looking across questioningly at her mother who immediately responded.

"Yes, Martha, I thought it would be a good idea. Janey seems to have some talent and don't worry about the expense. There is still some money in the kitty to fund it."

"Oh mum, you can't be spending all your savings on us."

"Fiddlesticks," said Nora standing up and taking their plates to the sink. "What's money for if you can't spend it? You can't take it with you" she added.

"Well, if you're sure mum. It's so generous of you."

As Martha went to help Nora with the washing up and Janey went to her room to finish her book the telephone rang.

"Hello," answered Nora wiping her hands on her apron.

"Hello, Nora," replied Meg. "How is little Brian now?"

"Oh, hello, Meg. He is resting in bed and just about back to normal. Little scallywag has just been asking for extra scones."

"Oh really, that's wonderful. He certainly gave us all a fright. Apparently from what I've heard the village has named him the miracle boy of Polperro!"

"Yes, that is a good name for him. It certainly was a close call. He scared the life out of us."

"Well, I just rang to see how he was. I won't keep you. You all must be wanting to relax after the drama. Let us know if you need anything won't you?"

"Yes, thanks Meg, thanks for your concern."

As Nora went back to the kitchen the telephone rang again.

"Hello," Nora answered.

"Hello, it's Dr. Young at Frimley sanitarium here. May I speak to Mrs. Johnson?"

Nora ran to find Martha who was now in the bathroom.

"Martha," she called through the door. "It's the sanitarium on the telephone. A doctor Young."

Martha flushed the toilet and raced to the telephone.

"Hello, Martha Johnson speaking," she said breathlessly.

"It's Edward Young here, Martha. I wanted to let you know that Tom has suffered a bit of a setback."

"Oh no," she exclaimed "What kind of a setback?"

"Well, we think it is some kind of infection. In cases such as his when there has been a pneumothorax performed there is always a risk of something like this occurring."

"Oh, will he be alright?" she asked anxiously winding the cord around her hand.

"He is stable at the moment but was in rather a delirium. I tried to call you earlier but there was no answer."

"Oh, really? Sorry, you couldn't get through, but we had rather a drama. My son had fallen over a cliff and we had been out most of the time searching for him."

"That's terrible. Is he alright now?"

"Yes, thank God he is. He had a bump on his forehead and a concussion."

"Well, you certainly are having your share of dramas Martha."

"Should I come and see him, doctor?" Martha asked. "I was due to leave here for London tomorrow morning."

"No, there is no urgency at the moment. We are keeping an eye on him but if there is any major change, I will let you know immediately."

"Thank you, Dr. I appreciate you contacting me. Please give Tom my love and I will see him as soon as I can."

"Will do. Goodbye Martha. I hope your boy improves. Take care of yourself."

Filled with anxiety, Martha told Nora about Tom's condition and then told Janey. Brian had fallen asleep, the soldiers with which he had been playing all fallen to the floor. Then, after dining on Nora's shepherd's pie, followed by jelly and custard, they all retired for an early night.

Sleep did not come easily for Martha. She tossed and turned thinking about what might have happened to her baby, broken and dead at the bottom of that cliff, and Tom seriously ill in that cold draughty sanitarium. She was still awake when the first seagulls' calls of the morning roused her to a new day in which she would leave her children in Cornwall and take the train back to London.

Chapter Fourteen

When Martha arrived home, the pervading quietude of the house had her wishing her children were not staying in Cornwall. Gathering the mail which proved to be mainly bills, she walked into the sitting room and turned on the radio for distraction, and then set about unpacking her luggage, putting her clean things away, and the rest into the basket to be washed. Then she put the kettle on to boil and looked in the cupboard for something to make for her tea. There were a few potatoes and a tin of spam. That will have to do until I go to the shops tomorrow.

As she filled the pan with water, she thought she should ring and see how Sylvia was and when she would be discharged from the hospital. Did she want to look after her mother-in-law in her convalescence? Could she really withstand the woman's snide comments on a daily basis? But she needed some extra money going by the bills which had been delivered, and it would save her actively looking for other employment. There was nothing for it but to take the bull by the horns and bite the bullet!

***

"Hello," Martha said as the hospital operator answered the telephone. "I was enquiring about Mrs. Johnson. Could you tell me if she is still a patient there?"

"One moment please," said the operator.

"Yes, she is still at the hospital. Would you like me to connect you to her room?"

Martha thought for a moment then said.

"No, it's alright thank you. I will ring later."

She put the telephone down and went back to the kitchen and dropped in the potatoes. I really don't feel inclined to talk to her right now she thought. Tomorrow is soon enough for that when I am more refreshed and have my thoughts collected. She sliced some spam onto the plate and then retrieved a jar of pickles from the cupboard.

The kettle boiled, she spooned some tea into the pot then after pouring the water, took it to the table. Then she drained the potatoes and put them on the plate with the spam. She just commenced eating when there was a knock on the door.

"Oh bother," she muttered to herself. "Just when I have sat down."

Opening the door she discovered it was Ethel from next door.

"Hello ducks, thought I heard you come home," said Ethel trying to muscle her way in.

"Oh, Ethel, yes, I haven't been home long. As a matter of fact, I have just sat down to eat."

"Oh, well then I will let you get on."

"Would you like to come in and have a cup of tea? I am only having some potatoes and spam until I can shop tomorrow."

"Alright ducks. Don't mind if I do. The bingo was cancelled tonight. Harry, the fellow who calls out the numbers took sick."

"Oh, that's a shame," said Martha leading the way into the kitchen.

"Yes, it is," replied Ethel sitting down. "Hope he comes good. There's a bit of gastro going around so I heard."

Martha poured the tea.

"Ah, it's good to take the weight off for a while," Ethel exclaimed. "Missed the bloomin' bus today and had to walk all the way to the doctors. It didn't do me bunions any good and that's a fact!"

Martha resumed eating.

"Are you sick Ethel?" she asked.

"No, not too sick ducks. Just the old ticker needed checking" she said slurping her tea.

She added, "Talking of sick, how's Tom?"

Martha swallowed a piece of potato.

"Oh, not too good I'm afraid. I had a call from a doctor at the sanitarium when I was at mum's. He contracted some sort of infection."

"Oh, blimey, thanks no good."

"No, it isn't, and then to top it all off we had a drama with Brian. He wandered off and got lost chasing Mum's pet goat. He ended up falling over the cliff, but his fall was stopped by a bush."

"What, Brian?" she cried "Oh my lord, the poor child. You must all have been beside yourselves with worry."

"Oh, God Ethel, it was terrible. I was terrified that something dreadful had happened. I had gone to have a rest and when I woke up no one was in the house. I went outside and found mum and Janey trying to find him. Then we decided to call the police who rounded up some local people to join in the search, but it was then too dark to see and they had to call off the search until first light" Martha continued, anxious to offload all the terrible events on to her neighbour who was relishing the gossip.

"And when did they find him?" asked Ethel eyes wide with wonder.

"At dawn, the next morning. He was lying caught on a bush protruding from the cliff."

With that, Martha, all the pent-up emotions spilling forth, started to cry as she thought of Tom and the moment when they discovered her baby.

"There, there ducks, you just let it all out," Ethel said going to Martha and putting her arms around her offering some comfort.

"It's all over now, all's well what ends well, isn't that what they say?"

Martha sniffed and agreed and told her that Brian had been named the miracle boy of Polperro. After another cup of tea Ethel, ensuring Martha was feeling better went next door. Lighting a cigarette, she sat down to ponder about her neighbour's misfortunes. She certainly would have something to relate to her cronies at the next bingo night and no mistake!

***

Her neighbour gone, Martha cleared away the plates and washed up. Then turning off the lights and the wireless took herself to bed.

All too soon the sun's rays crept through the curtains and Martha lay in bed wondering how her children were, especially Brian and also her darling Tom. Even though she felt thoroughly exhausted, she thought she must try to see him today. There was a train at 9:30 pm. If she hurried she could catch it but then she would not have time to talk to Sylvia; she would keep until tomorrow. There was nothing more important now than seeing Tom.

She had a quick wash, a bite of toast, and a cup of tea then, throwing on some clothes and applying some lipstick, she grabbed her bag and was out the door just managing to catch the bus to the station.

As she waited for the ancient lift to transport her to Tom's floor, she began to feel rather lightheaded. I hope I'm not coming down with something she thought. That would be all I need on top of everything that had been happening. She walked into the room to find a nurse taking Tom's temperature. He did not look at all well, his skin had a greyish tinge and he seemed to have lost more weight.

"Hello Mrs. Johnson," she said as she kept her fingers on Tom's pulse.

"Hello," Martha said as she sat down on the chair. "How is he?"

"His temperature is a bit elevated at the moment. The doctor is due to see him shortly."

She hurried out to complete her rounds.

Martha took his hand and said, "Tom, dear it's me, Martha."

Opening his eyes Martha detected a slight smile appearing on his poor gaunt face.

"Just rest dear. Don't try to talk. The nurse said the doctor is on his way to see you."

Just then doctor Young strode into the room.

Martha stood up to greet him and as she did so little black spots appeared before her eyes. Then she was aware of her forehead resting on her knees and Edward Young was propping her up.

"What happened?" she asked.

"You fainted, Martha," he replied as he poured some water into a glass and gave her some to sip.

He helped her to the chair and then she felt a cold sweat breaking out on her top lip and forehead.

"Oh, sorry. I'm so embarrassed," she said taking her handkerchief from her bag to wipe away the moisture.

Edward replied.

"No need to feel embarrassed. Have you eaten properly this morning? Sometimes a faint occurs when one hasn't had enough to eat."

Martha told him how she had been rushing around, going to and coming back from Cornwall, about the mishap with Brian, and the worry about Tom's latest infection, and that she had not had time to eat much before she had to catch the train.

He said he would have one of the nurses bring her a sandwich and a cup of tea. In answer to her question about Tom's condition, he apprised her of the situation which did not sound at all positive.

"Sorry for the bad news, Martha," he said. "But you have to realise that because of Tom's weakened constitution he does not have the resilience to fight infection. We are doing all we can for him, but I'm afraid the outlook is not good."

Martha took Tom's scrawny hand and rested her head on the blanket, tears flowing freely, she heard the wheezing noises of her husband as he struggled to draw breath into his damaged lungs.

As Edward patted her shoulder a nurse appeared carrying a tray on which was a sandwich and a pot of tea.

"Here we are then," she said setting it down on the table and scuttled out as fast as she had come in.

"Thank you for everything you've done, doctor," said Martha trying to put her face into some semblance of order, knowing she must look a fright but not really caring anyway.

"Call me Edward, Martha."

"Alright," she said. "Edward. Do you know how much time Tom has?" she asked crumpling the now wet handkerchief in her hands.

"No, not really. It's a case of taking one day at a time. Sometimes the patient rallies. I'm afraid we will just have to wait and see."

As she took a bite of the sandwich which was cheese and pickle Edward told her he had to finish his rounds but he would come and look in on Tom before she left for London.

As Martha ate, her mind was filled with thoughts of Tom's ultimate demise and of her children in Cornwall, in particular Brian, who had escaped the jaws of death by a fraction. She stroked Tom's gaunt cheek and put her arms around him and prayed that if God had to take her husband he would not suffer much pain.

Chapter Fifteen

Helen was humming to herself as she cut around the edges of the pastry. She was making a lord Woolton pie which happened to be Mike's favourite. Since he had been staying for dinner more often Helen found that she rather enjoyed cooking, whereas before when it was just her and Val, the making of meals had become a bit tedious. She found that she looked forward to his visits more and more and was so pleased that her mother looked even more forward as it was the highlight of her day.

Mike had been visiting the library and procuring books which he knew Val was interested in, Somerset Maugham being one of her favourites, in particular his short stories which Mike had ploughed through. Now the current book was *The Vessel of Wrath,* which he had managed to reserve as there was only one copy available at the library.

Helen put the pie in the oven and then taking off her apron, went to do something with her hair. I must try and go to the hairdresser soon she thought as she brushed and put a kirbigrip in her hair. There was a lady from the council who popped in occasionally to sit with Val if Helen had to go out. Lately, she found that she was looking after her appearance more. I wonder if that has anything to do with Mike's visits she wondered? He really was such a nice man, kind and considerate. He certainly did not deserve such treatment by his wife after what he had been through in the war. She applied some lipstick and then went to see about tidying her mother for Mike's arrival.

"There mum," she said after she had changed Val's bedjacket for a fresh one which was a pale lemon satin edged with white lace.

"You look fit for an audience with the Queen."

Val's eyes lit up with that announcement.

"Mike will be here soon and after we will have our tea," Helen told her.

"I've made a nice lord Woolton pie for us" she added.

As she straightened the eiderdown there was the familiar knock on the door.

"That will be your reader mum, right on time as always," Helen said walking from the room.

"Hello Mike, how are you?" said Helen opening the door.

"Hello Helen, good to see you again. How's mum today?"

"She's good. Looking forward to her session," Helen replied as she led the way.

"Well, don't you look a sight for sore eyes?" Mike told Val as he stepped into her room.

Helen said, "I just told her she looked fit for an audience with the Queen!"

They both laughed and Val's eyes crinkled with amusement.

Helen went to the kitchen and poured three glasses of sherry which she placed on the tray and carried it to Val's room.

"Here are our pre-dinner drinks," she said handing a glass to Mike. She sat down next to Val and helped her sip the sherry then she clinked glasses with Mike.

"Cheers," he said. "Just what I needed I must say. It's been rather a day," said Mike.

"Busy?" asked Helen giving Val another sip as she noticed her eyes focusing on the glass

"Yes, it was rather. I didn't know if I was Arthur or Martha. Nothing seemed to go right. I couldn't get the figures to balance, and to top it all off, the receptionist phoned in sick so I ended up answering the phone," he said downing the last drop of sherry.

"Oh, poor you," said Helen. "I remember days like that at the hospital, especially on night shift when you felt so tired you thought your feet would not carry you another step."

Mike replied, "The days in the lives of the worker!"

Helen put the now empty glasses on the tray and took them back to the kitchen for washing then, taking the paper, went to the sitting room to catch up on the news while her mother was being read to. But Helen could not seem to concentrate on what she was reading. Her thoughts were in the form of one man who was presently in her mother's room. What a silly fool she thought. He wouldn't want someone like me sequestered here, a spinster living with an old mother, having not had any boyfriends to speak of.

She thought of the times before her mother had her illness, of the times as a child growing up in Chester, when her baby brother in his second year had been taken by a disease called diphtheria. Her father, inconsolable at the loss of his only son, had wailed and thrown himself at the tiny coffin as it was lowered into the ground. Then, soon after, moving them to Ealing where he worked in a branch insurance office, far away from the terrible memory: then, fleeing to the great war, not caring if he lived or died, such was the depth of his despair.

How she had even then, as young as she was, tried to support her mother through that traumatic time. The terrible times when she came home from school to find her mother prostrate on the floor, the empty bottles of gin on the sink, testament to her inability to cope with the sad circumstances of her life.

They ran to the neighbour next door so between them they could lift her mother up the stairs and into bed, where the effects of the drink would hopefully wear off by the morning. Helen would get herself up and, more often than not, arrive at school with an empty stomach, such was the state of the food supply in the house.

And school was not much better as she had been teased mercilessly by some of her classmates due to her unkempt appearance: the teachers caning her for not submitting her homework in time. Her lack of friends had contributed to her introversion, and she turned to books for companionship frequenting the library whenever she could and finding that she enjoyed reading about the lives of nurses, especially Florence Nightingale.

Many a night she would lay in her bed thinking how she would love to walk through a ward, lantern in her hand, caring for the sick in her care. But there was one night when any such thought was absent.

Her mother, to make ends meet had taken in a lodger, one Douglas Lynch. He was a simpering, fawning milksop whom Helen disliked totally, as he took any opportunity to sidle up and rub against her. His sweaty, fat hands were like lumps of clay trying to paw her whenever he had the chance.

This had happened when Helen was in bed, her door unlocked, and her mother sleeping off another binge. It had been two weeks before her twelfth birthday when he had put his fat hand over her mouth to stop her screams. When she had felt her nightdress lifted and her panties pulled down and something hard trying to go into her. A thrusting and him panting, then, left alone in her bed, terrified beyond belief, she had felt a sticky wetness on her stomach and leaking onto the sheet.

Afterward, him telling her it was their little secret, and if she breathed a word to anyone, she, along with her mother, would be killed. She told her mother how she disliked this lodger, but her reply was that he was a good, god-fearing man attending chapel every Sunday and she did not understand her daughter's intense dislike of him.

Thereafter, Helen made sure she was never alone with him and always locked her bedroom door every night. The experience had permanently scarred her making it difficult to form relationships with men.

It was not until many years later when she had left home and commenced her nursing career that she had told her mother of the traumatic experience in her childhood.

Her mother, shocked to the core, had gathered Helen in her arms and wept uncontrollably both for the loss of her daughter's childhood innocence and the fact that she did not heed her warnings.

When her father had eventually come home from the war he was a shadow of his former self. Suffering from the effects of the dreadful mustard gas and shrapnel embedded in his back, he was incarcerated in the Clapham Auxiliary Medical Hospital, where he was treated for his injuries as well as for venereal disease. His time there was short-lived as he succumbed to his injuries a few months later, Helen and her mother having visited him a couple of days before. That day was one of rain and lashing wind as they struggled aboard two buses, Helen's mother not quite recovered from another session with the bottle, complaining of a headache. Helen did her best to keep the umbrella from blowing inside out as the wind howled and the rain bucketed down in sheets. They eventually arrived at the hospital like two drowned rats only to be told that the visiting hour had nearly expired.

They hurried to a ward filled with injured soldiers some crying in agony, others unconscious to pain: their friend, morphine, now having taken effect. Eventually, they found Helen's father trying to inhale air through a mask, his face a sickly yellow colour, covered in blisters and emitting a dreadful odour.

Afterward to be told that venereal disease had that effect, and his time was limited. That was too much for Helen's mother who flung herself on the bed, and with hands thumping her husband's body screaming.

"You went with tarts and look at you now!"

Slumping to the floor, the orderlies were summoned, and she and Helen were escorted out of the ward, where they were offered some tea and time for her mother to compose herself before they had to set off for home.

Helen's memory of her father's funeral was hazy. Two aunts of her mother had appeared from Brighton and had taken control of proceedings. They had quickly sized up the situation regarding her mother and the demon drink. Her memory was of being tucked up in bed and being brought crustless sandwiches made with cucumber and glasses of lemonade. She was admonished to stay there until she had her strength back as, up until then, her energy had been expended trying to look after her mother.

She had been so grateful to those women who had alighted like angels, albeit in black, and taken her and her mother under their wings. They tidied the house moving around as though on wheels, beating the rugs, changing the sheets, and pouring down the sink any bottles of alcohol they found. Nourishing meals were cooked, and although there were some setbacks, it was not long until Helen's mother had some pink in her cheeks and a bit more spring in her step all due to the tireless efforts of the aunts.

When it was time for Helen to leave home to study nursing it was decided that one of the aunts would stay to keep her eye on her mother so Helen could concentrate on her studies, and not be burdened with worry. Helen had been forever grateful to those aunts for lifting that weight off her shoulders to pursue her nursing career, until the day that her mother fell ill due to the alcohol she had consumed over the years.

"What does a chap have to do to get some tea around here?"

Startled from her reverie at the sound of Mike's voice Helen leapt up off the lounge.

"Oh, sorry I was in a trance. I must have nodded off for a while," said Helen patting her hair and straightening her skirt.

"No harm done. I was only joking. That pie is smelling delicious. Come on and I'll help you serve," Mike said as led the way into the kitchen.

Helen took the pie from the oven and cutting three pieces placed them on the plates then Mike procured some cutlery and between the two of them transported the lot to the invalid's room. They commenced eating, Mike commenting it was the most delicious pie he had eaten in a long while. Helen spooned some pie into Val's mouth with the majority of it trickling down her chin and that was the moment Helen's feelings for Mike took quite a turn. Totally unprompted, Mike leapt up and with a flick of the napkin wiped Val's face clean.

Chapter Sixteen

When Edward had come around to check on Tom, he had again discovered Martha fainted and nauseous on the floor and had quickly contacted his mother to enquire if she could perhaps rest there in a homely environment away from the atmosphere of the hospital. Millicent was only too pleased to help the lady in distress and had arrived soon after with an invitation for her to spend the night. She whisked Martha away to a beautiful white cottage tucked away in the village of Frimley Green. Martha felt rather embarrassed about feeling ill and was most apologetic for inconveniencing everyone, especially Edward's mother. She had said it was no trouble at all and was glad to be doing something useful for a change.

As she reclined on the chaise longue, a blanket over her and a cup of sugared tea and a biscuit by her side, Martha admired the pretty sitting room in which she found herself. There was a grand piano at the far end on which were various photos among them being Edward as a child and at his graduation, mortar board atop his head. There were photos of presumably his poor deceased brother, Jeff also as a child and one in which he looked resplendent in an officer's uniform. She noticed the Persian rugs on the floor and a crystal vase of lilies perched on a gleaming gate leg table, while the white walls boasted pictures of sleepy meadows with fat cows gently grazing. An escritoire resided in a corner and there were French doors opening onto a garden while a fireplace stacked with wood ensured the room would be very cosy on a cold winter's day.

"Feeling better dear?" asked Millicent as she came back into the room with a cup of tea in her hand.

"Oh, much better now thank you. I'm really very grateful for your kindness. I don't want to be a bother," said Martha taking another sip of tea, the sweetness just what she needed, restoring her energy.

"Nonsense, as I said before, it's a nice diversion." She sat down on the sofa.

"Now." she added, "Tell me about yourself. Edward told me about your dear husband's illness and his time in the war. Have you any children?"

"Yes, I do. A boy and a girl. Brian is five and Janey is twelve. At the moment, they are spending the school holidays with their nanna in Cornwall."

"Oh, that's lovely. It's nice to have a pigeon pair. I'll bet the young fellow keeps you on your toes to say nothing of his nanna!"

Martha put her cup down.

"Yes, he does, as a matter of fact, we nearly lost him recently."

"Oh, what happened?" asked Millicent as she sat on the sofa.

"Well, his nanna lives on a farm on top of a cliff in Polperro and the pet goat escaped. Brian had set off after it and the two of them fell over the cliff."

"Oh, my heavens!" exclaimed Millicent.

"Was he alright?"

"Yes, thank goodness, he was saved by an overhanging bush and escaped with only a bump to the head and a concussion. The goat I'm afraid is no longer."

"Oh, you poor dear. You have had some bad luck."

"Yes, they say things come in threes. I'm now wondering what the third will be."

"Yes, I have heard that. One never knows what life will throw at one."

Martha said, "Did Edward tell you that I met your sister Joan?"

"Yes, he did. That was a coincidence, wasn't it?"

"It certainly was. She and I had a bite to eat a few weeks ago. She seems a lovely person."

"Yes, Joan is a good egg. Mind you, we did not get on as youngsters. It's only now that we are older, that we have become good friends."

Martha said, "I don't wish to pry but Joan told me about the tragedy in Edward's life."

"Yes, poor Edward. It was a dreadful time losing his wife to that terrible disease. It's only recently that his old spark has returned."

Martha drank the last drop of her tea and as Millicent walked over to take her cup to the kitchen said.

"Well, it's just us for supper tonight. Charles is away for a few days at a medical conference in London. So, we will have some soup here in front of the fire."

"Oh, that sounds lovely," said Martha adding, "I presume Charles is your husband?"

"Oh yes, silly me. I should have said."

"And is he a doctor too?" asked Martha not wanting to appear ignorant

"Yes, but he is semi-retired, just does the odd op. He still likes to keep his hand in" replied Millicent.

Martha asked, "What does he specialise in?"

"He is a facio maxillary surgeon and needless to say there is an overwhelming amount of work. All those poor souls with their faces disfigured or missing. It doesn't bear thinking about."

She stood up.

"Now, I think it's time I lit the fire. When the sun goes down it tends to become a little chilly in these parts. We can have our soup here where it is cosier. I'm afraid I become rather casual when Charles is away. One tends to tire of setting up in the dining room every night. Just between you and me" she whispered conspiratorially" Sometimes I rather look forward to making do with a boiled egg and toast soldiers!"

Martha smiled in agreement thinking how much she was liking this woman and could not help comparing her to Tom's mother whom she still had not contacted.

After lighting the fire, Millicent walked to the gramophone and selected a record. Soon the pervading warmth and the strains of a Hayden sonata filled the room blotting out Martha's anxieties as she lay back and let it all wash over her.

"There," said Millicent. "This should warm the cockles of the heart," as she put the bowls of steaming soup on the table along with a plate of bread and butter.

"Oh, thank you. It smells delicious. What sort of soup is it?" Martha asked as she made room for Millicent on the sofa.

"It's potato and leek. Gwyneth the daily made it."

"Oh, I see," said Martha thinking what a life some people lead having a daily make their soup.

"Well, it's very tasty," commented Martha after she had tried some.

They ate their soup to the sound of another composer, Bach, and Martha felt that she was actually enjoying it: it was really quite soothing. She and Tom usually listened to jazz or whatever the popular music was on the wireless and they had never bothered very much with the classics. However, they had attended an opera or two before they married so were not totally uncultured.

"So, Martha," said Millicent after they had finished the soup and she was pouring some coffee. "Where is home for you?"

"We live in Ealing, not far from Joan's actually."

"Oh, that's right. I seem to remember Joan telling me."

"And are your husband's parents still living?"

Martha took the cup of coffee from Millicent and added a teaspoon of sugar.

"His father is deceased, but his mother is still alive. She lives in Belgravia."

"Oh," exclaimed Millicent. "Nice area."

"Yes" answered Martha "It is very nice. She has quite a large house. Far too big for one person I think but she has lived there all her life and would not want to move anywhere else. But she recently had a fall and broke her hip, so she has been in hospital. She is due to go to a convalescent home, but she would rather be cared for at home. As a matter of fact, she has asked me if I would be her carer."

Millicent put down her coffee.

"And would you do that?" she asked.

"Well, I have been thinking about it. The trouble is Millicent, may I call you that?"

"Please," she said.

"Well, the trouble is, she is rather a difficult person and doesn't get on with us especially Tom whom she has never forgiven for going to the war and contracting his illness and always mentions it whenever we see her."

"Oh, she does not sound very nice at all. If I was you I would tell her to look for someone else or go to the convalescent home."

"Yes, I have thought of that but, with Tom the way he is I really need some sort of paid work."

"I see. Well, I will keep my nose to the ground. I know the hospital where Charles operates sometimes has positions vacant in the administration department. Do you have any qualifications?"

"Yes, I was a legal secretary before I was married although I found the work rather dry, typing contracts and documents. I suppose I rather fell into it; I should have pursued a career in nursing or something else to do with a hospital, medical records for instance. At one stage that was an option" Martha reflected sipping her coffee.

"Well, there you are then," said Millicent settling further back into the sofa. "It sounds as though a position in a hospital would be just the thing for you."

They finished their coffee and Millicent led the way upstairs to a bedroom in which Martha would stay the night until she would be driven to the station the following morning. Then she went off to find Martha a nightdress and came back with a long blue number bedecked with frills and bows.

"This should fit you," Millicent said as she put it on the bed.

"Now, there is a towel and a toothbrush in the bathroom which you'll find just along the passage."

"Oh, thank you for everything Millicent. You have been so terribly generous. I am very appreciative."

"Nonsense. It has been my pleasure. Now you just have a good sleep and after breakfast, I shall drive you to the station," she gave Martha a peck on the cheek. "Goodnight, my dear, sleep well."

Martha wished her hostess a good night also and after she had gone Martha made her way to the bathroom where she found the toothbrush. She washed her face with the bar of perfumed soap which rested on a pale blue dish then proceeded to brush her teeth. She used the lavatory, then tiptoed back to the bedroom and, after changing into the borrowed nightdress climbed into bed.

Lying there, Martha thought back over the day. She could not believe that she was spending the night with the mother of Tom's doctor, Edward. How embarrassed she had felt fainting and being nauseous like that! I must try to look after myself a bit better and not be rushing around so much but I had to see Tom.

Oh, my Tom she thought, how are you now? Please don't die and leave me and our children! Please get well! Then the pillow and the front of her borrowed nightdress had become wet with her tears as they had flowed unchecked, dribbling down her cheeks and onto her neck when sleep finally came to claim her.

Chapter Seventeen

The first thing Martha did when she arrived home from Frimley was to telephone the sanitarium to ascertain Tom's condition. She was advised that it was unchanged, and he was as well as could be expected so somewhat reassured she then rang the hospital to see how Sylvia was.

"Connecting you now," said the operator as she put the call through to Sylvia's room.

"Hello" answered Sylvia.

"Oh, hello Sylvia, it's Martha speaking. How are you?"

"Well, it's about time I heard from you. I could be dead and buried and not a word from the lot of you. It's a nice state of affairs!" she railed.

"I'm sorry I haven't been in touch sooner, Sylvia but I have had some dramas of my own to worry about," replied Martha wishing she did not have to listen to her admonishments.

"Dramas, what dramas?" she remonstrated.

Martha rubbed her forehead.

"Well, Tom has taken a turn for the worst. It seems he contracted an infection from the operation. The doctor said he may rally but the prognosis at the moment is not good."

Not hearing any response she ploughed on.

"And there was a near tragedy with Brian at mum's. He was chasing the pet goat and ended up falling over the cliff."

"Falling over the cliff?" cried her mother-in-law "Wasn't anyone looking after him for heaven's sake?"

"Well, we weren't aware that he had gone missing until it became dark. Nora was in the studio with Janey, and I was having a lie down. We had to call the police to search for him as well as the local people and it wasn't until dawn the next morning that they found him saved by an overhanging bush."

"Well, I must say!" Sylvia exclaimed "What that boy needs is better discipline and with no father around one can see he is doing as he pleases. It would not have happened in my day I can assure you!"

Martha was finding the conversation very draining and could not believe that she had not even asked after the welfare of her son.

"Brian only sustained a mild concussion and a bump to his forehead," she told her.

"Well, I hope that is a lesson to him" she railed.

"Now, have you thought about my proposition?" she added.

Martha expecting the question said, "Actually I have thought about it Sylvia but I'm afraid the answer is no."

"No? But you have the time. The children are at Nora's and then they will be at school."

"I know but I am not a professional carer and I think you would be better off at a convalescent home where you will be expertly taken care of. However, I do thank you for the offer."

"Well, if that's how you feel there is no more to be said on the matter. I will have to make other arrangements."

"Very well, I hope you will be able to sort things out. Take care of yourself and I will give Tom your love."

"Yes, you do that. Goodbye."

Martha hung up the telephone and sat there thoroughly exhausted but at the same time relieved that she had told her mother-in-law she was declining the offer of being her carer. She got up and went to the kitchen to make herself a cup of tea. Then she thought she must go to the shops and refill the pantry. I must make myself something nourishing to gain my strength back and not be eating on the run as I have been lately.

Waiting for the kettle to boil, she sat down in the kitchen and, taking some paper and a pencil made a list of things to buy: Potatoes, mincemeat, onions, beans, carrots, eggs, bread, butter, and lard. That should tide me over for a couple of days. The kettle boiled, she made the tea and, finding a biscuit which Brian had not managed to eat settled down with the newspaper which she had bought on the way from the station.

After her sustaining tea break, she decided to do some washing. As there was not much, it was not worth lighting the copper so she boiled some water to pour into the dish in which she would hand wash the few dirty items. Pouring in the soap flakes Martha thought how heartless was Tom's mother. Not even commenting on his condition! She really was the limit!

Just then the telephone rang jolting her from her thoughts.

"Hello," she answered.

"Hello Marth, it's Helen."

"Oh hello, good to hear from you. How are you?"

"Oh, I'm fine."

"And Val?"

"Much the same although she seems more cheerful since Mike has started visiting."

"I'll bet she loves it."

"Yes, she certainly does, and I don't mind telling you I rather look forward to him coming over too."

"Oh, is that so?"

Martha settled herself in the chair ready for a pleasant interlude with her friend.

"Yes, that is so. You know Marth, I think Mike and I have a connection. I have never felt like this about anyone else. As you know, I have always kept my distance from the opposite sex but with Mike it is different. I can't explain it."

Martha listened with a sense of happiness for her dear friend whom she knew had experienced quite a traumatic childhood. Now was it possible that she had at last connected with someone who could bring some joy into her life albeit at this late stage and did Mike have the same feeling for her friend?

"Well, it sounds as though everyone is benefiting," said Martha as an errant fly landed on her lap. She flicked it off.

"But enough of me. How are things with you? How is poor Tom and did the children go to Nora's?"

"Well, Tom is not good at all Helen" she replied.

"He had a turn for the worst. Apparently, he caught an infection after the operation and was rather delirious. The doctor said he may rally but because of his weakened constitution, he did not hold much hope for his recovery. We just have to take it one day at a time I'm afraid."

"Oh, Marth, so sorry, that's terrible."

"Yes, it's hit me rather hard. I also had the fright of my life with Brian."

"Oh, what happened with him?"

"Well, we all arrived at mum's and after having something to eat mum and Janey went into the studio. I went to have a lie down and must have dropped off to sleep. The next thing I knew mum and Janey were up the field trying to find Brian. It turned out that he went looking for the goat which had escaped through the fence and in the dark he managed to fall over the cliff."

"What?" cried Helen.

"Yes, he fell over but was miraculously saved by an overhanging bush. The police found him the next day and thank God he came away with only a concussion and a bump on the forehead."

"My heavens, Marth he was lucky. I couldn't imagine how worried you must have been. You must have been nearly demented."

"Yes, it was terrible. I could have lost my little boy," tears started to well in Martha's eyes as she recounted the terrible episode.

"Oh, Marth. But thank the lord he is alright. They say these things are sent to try us," Helen said trying to comfort her friend as she detected the distress in her voice.

"Yes, you're right, at least it is all behind us now. They named him the miracle boy of Polperro," she added.

"Well, he certainly is that by all accounts!" said Helen.

"Did I tell you about Tom's doctor, Edward Young?" asked Martha.

"No, what about him?"

"Well, I ran into his aunt Joan on the train when I was coming back from visiting Tom one day and we started talking. She told me that her nephew worked at the sanitarium and his brother was killed in France."

"Go on," said Helen all ears to the news.

"Well, to make a long story short I have met Edward a couple of times as he has been looking in on Tom, and the last time which was a day ago when I embarrassed myself by fainting in his presence."

"Oh, then what happened?"

"Well, he could see I was not in a fit state to travel all that way on the train so he rang his mother who lives at Frimley to ask her if she would take me to her place so I could recover sufficiently to travel home. It turned out that this lovely woman took me into her home, gave me tea, or supper as she called it, and put me to bed for the night, driving me to the station and I arrived home this morning."

"Oh, for goodness sake. How incredible."

"Yes, I still can't believe it at all. I was terribly embarrassed about the whole episode, but she took it all in her stride and said it gave her something to do as she is finding it hard dealing with the loss of her other son."

"And was her husband around at all?" asked Helen.

"No, he was at a medical conference in London. She told me he is a facio maxillary surgeon but is semi-retired, just does the odd operation."

"I see. Well, that is a story and a half I must say."

Martha then said, "I rang the witch of Belgravia this morning."

"And what did she have to say for herself?"

"She's still in the hospital but is being discharged shortly. She had a go at me for not contacting her sooner, but I told her of my dramas. Do you know, Helen that she did not even comment on her son's condition and all she had to say about Brian was that he needed more discipline, never mind that he could have lost his life."

"That woman, Martha. I wouldn't give her the time of day. I hope you told her you wouldn't be looking after her."

"Yes, I certainly did. She said she would be making arrangements with a convalescent home."

"Just as well. They can put up with her then."

"Helen, I have been thinking, now I am not going to look after her, I might investigate getting a part-time position in one of the hospitals. You know I have always had a penchant for the hospital environment and when I was talking to Edward's mother, she reinforced the idea. I never really enjoyed working for the legal profession."

"That sounds like a great idea Marth," said Helen. "Do you want me to contact any of my old workmates from St Barts to see if they know of any positions?"

"Oh, well if you wouldn't mind, that would be a start, thanks ever so Helen."

"Don't mention it. Well, I had better let you get on. Can't be nattering all day," said Helen.

"Yes, I suppose so. I have some hand washing to finish then I was going to the shops for some supplies. Give my love to Val and also Mike."

"Will do, come over one night for tea."

"I have a better idea. How about I come over and mind Val and you and Mike can go out for a bite together?"

"Oh, really? Oh, that would be perfect. Thanks a million, Marth."

"You just nominate a night, and I will be there."

"Alright, I will run it past Mike and let you know. Maybe Friday would be good as he would not have to get up for work the next day."

"Sounds good, I will plan for Friday, and if it's not suitable just let me know."

"Ok, thanks again Marth, take care of yourself and love to Tom and the children. Bye."

Martha finished the washing and after pegging it on the line took her basket and her list and made her way to the shops with a somewhat lighter heart than what she had only a few hours earlier.

Chapter Eighteen

The picture was not turning out as well as she hoped it would. Janey tore the paper off the easel in frustration and went into the kitchen where she found her nanna in a floury apron kneading some dough for the pie they would have for their tea.

"What's up pet?" asked Nora.

Janey sat down and started winding a tendril of hair around her finger.

"My painting isn't going right nan. I have tried to do as you said but the perspective is all wrong."

"Just leave it for a while and I will come and help you with it after I have finished this."

Nora placed the rolled dough on top of the meat and took the knife to cut around it to fit the dish.

"I already tore the paper off," said Janey looking at Nora rather shame-faced.

"Well, there is plenty more paper to go on with, so nothing to worry about, eh?"

Janey nodded and then asked Nora how long it had taken her to become a good artist and if she would ever become as good as her. Nora told her it takes years of practice and patience, but the main thing was to enjoy the process. Not everyone had the talent to be a Van Gogh or a Monet. Janey asked who were they and then Nora explained about the Impressionists and the famous paintings they had produced. She told her she had a book about them and when the pie was installed in the oven, she took

Annette Creswell

Janey to the bookcase to see if they could unearth the book. After looking along the shelves finally, the book was found, and dusting it off with her apron set it down on the table which she had cleared of the flour. They sat down and opened the book and Janey was transfixed by the beautiful pictures of sunflowers and French fields which seemed to jump out at her as she turned the pages, one picture in particular at which she exclaimed.

"Oh, nan, grandma has this one. I have told her I like it as it seems to remind me of Cornwall when the sea is churned up by the storms."

Nora looked at what Janey was pointing at. It happened to be Turner's, Dawn After the Wreck.

"Are you sure Janey?" asked Nora thinking surely the woman has a print and not the original.

"Yes, quite sure Nan. It's on the wall in her foyer."

Nora was taken aback by this. If that woman has an original, she must be worth more than anyone imagines and still she cannot bear to part with any of her money to help her own flesh and blood. It was unbelievable!

"What are you looking at?" asked Brian mud all over his pants, coming in from feeding Harold some vegetable scraps.

"We're looking at paintings done a long time ago Brian," said Nora. "And look at the state of those pants. You always manage to get yourself in a state. I don't know how your mother must keep up with the washing! I hope you wiped those feet of yours before you came in."

Brian looking sheepish and turning red said he tried to but did not think he was successful. Nora, looking at the floor that she had cleaned not long ago agreed with her grandson and shaking her head took the mop and cleaned the worst of the mud.

"Never mind, it's only good old dirt after all, isn't it pet?"

Page | 160

Brian relieved that he was not going to be roused on as would have been the case if it had been Grandmother Johnson, skipped over to the tin and helped himself to a biscuit.

"Now, only one mind, Brian otherwise you won't eat your tea," admonished his nanna.

"What's for tea nan?" asked Brian stuffing the biscuit into his mouth.

"We're having a nice cottage pie pet."

"And are we having anything for afters?"

"Yes, we will have some tinned pears and cream."

"I love those. Sometimes ma buys them for us," said Brian as he ran off to his room to finish his game of soldiers. Janey and Nora continued looking through the art book and Nora thought how well Brian was looking now after his accident, his colour had returned to his cheeks and the lump on his forehead had gone down considerably.

After they had their tea Nora suggested that tomorrow if it was a fine day, they might take a picnic down to the beach. This suggestion was met with approval by her grandchildren especially Brian who was envisioning splashing in the waves even though it was probably going to be too chilly for that.

Janey asked if Nora was bringing her easel and paints and if she was Janey might do some painting also and it was decided that the two artists would indeed take their easels and do some sketching at the beach. Nora hoped that going there would not bring back any bad memories for Brian, but he seemed to have adjusted since his fall and had been philosophical about the demise of poor Lucy.

So, the next day the threesome was up bright and early to greet the new day which dawned with a promise of brilliant sunshine. After a hearty breakfast of bacon and freshly laid eggs, Nora retrieved the picnic basket and commenced making some sandwiches which she wrapped in greaseproof paper. A few apples and a bottle of lemonade which she had made in preparation for the children's visit were added along with some fruit cake, and the lot was covered by a tea towel. Then she went to the linen press and found a blanket for them to sit on and some towels with which to dry themselves if they felt inclined for a paddle.

"Janey, Brian," called Nora.

Brian came bounding down the stairs carrying some of his soldiers.

"Are you taking those pets?" asked Nora.

"Yes, nan I'm going to build a fort in the sand," replied Brian as he put the soldiers on the table.

"Where's Janey then?" asked Nora.

"Don't know. She might be in the lavatory," said Brian as he sat down and peered under the tea towel to see what was on offer for their picnic.

"Now, get your head out of that basket, young man. That is our picnic for later and nothing is to be eaten before," admonished Nora as she went up the stairs in search of Janey.

"Janey," called her nanna. "Are you in the lavatory?"

"Yes, nanna," Janey replied in a trembling voice.

"Are you alright pet?" Nora asked through the door.

Janey replied, "I'm not sure nanna. I think there is something wrong with me."

Nora asked if she could come in and opening the door found Janey sitting on the lavatory with her panties on the floor stained with blood.

"Oh, you sweet child," said Nora going over and putting her arm around her shoulders. "It's alright, you have what is known as the curse. It means that you are now a woman. Didn't your mother tell you anything about it?"

Janey sniffed and said no she wasn't told anything, and she thought she might have had some awful sickness. Nora took the soiled underwear to soak and after she had Janey cleaned, she went to the cupboard. She found some old scraps of a towel and two safety pins which she gave to Janey showing her how to put it on.

"Nan," called Brian. "When are we going?"

"In a minute, Brian. I'm just doing something with Janey. We won't be long."

"Do I have to wear this all day?" asked Janey feeling somewhat uncomfortable with the bulky contraption between her legs.

"Yes, pet until we can go to the chemist and buy some pads which will be more comfortable."

"Can we go now before our picnic then?" asked Janey with a concerned look on her face.

"Yes, pet we will go now. I will just get my purse. You go out to the car and take Brian with you."

Brian jumped up off the chair and grabbed his soldiers ready to scoot off to the beach.

"Brian, we have to go and buy something at the shop first before we go to the beach. Come out to the car and wait for nanna. She's just getting her purse."

"What do we have to buy at the shop Janey? Some more biscuits?" asked her brother skipping ahead and banging the two soldiers together in a mock battle.

"No, it's not more biscuits, Brian. It's something personal for me" replied Janey opening the car door and climbing inside.

Brian climbed in after her.

"What's personal?" he asked.

"Never mind, you wouldn't understand."

Nora came and started the car, and they were on their way to the village. Nora managed to park in a spot right outside the chemist and leaving the children in the car walked into the shop to buy Janey's supplies.

She came out with a parcel wrapped in brown paper.

"What's that?" asked Brian.

"None of your business," said Janey as Nora placed the parcel on the seat next to her.

"Nan" whined Brian "Janey won't tell me what you bought for her."

"Oh, Brian," replied his nanna as she started the car "It's something just for ladies. When you are older you will know all about it."

Brian turned his face to the window and thought the world was a funny place. First, his father had to sleep in that cold hospital with all the windows open, and now only ladies were bought mysterious parcels from chemist shops! These adults surely were a strange lot!

They arrived home and after Nora had shown Janey how to put on the special belt around her waist and pinned the pad in place, they were ready to embark on their picnic.

"Nan, my stomach hurts as well," said Janey.

"Does it pet? Well, unfortunately, that is all part of this event. It means that your body is preparing for when you have a baby. It's the lining of the womb which comes away every month if there is no baby to be nourished and sometimes you feel some cramping" Nora explained.

"Do you still have this curse nan?"

"Oh, no, not now thank goodness. My days of having it are well past. Usually, it ceases when a woman turns 50. It is called menopause. Sometimes it happens earlier which is called premature menopause and sometimes it happens after 50, it all depends on the family's history."

"Oh, I see," said Janey.

"I know it's a lot for you to take in when you weren't prepared for it. I suppose your mother didn't expect you to reach puberty this early. That's why she did not tell you anything. Now, do you still want to go to the beach, pet? We can always go tomorrow if you want to stay in bed today."

"No, I'll be alright. I'll lie on the sand and read my book. I don't think I feel like painting today."

"Ok, you bring your book and relax. The sun should make you feel a bit better and there will be plenty of time for you to paint. If you still don't feel well, you can always come back and rest."

So, the threesome made their way down to the beach. Nora carrying her easel and a bag holding her paints, Janey carrying the basket, her book, and the blanket, and Brian coming up the rear with the towels and his beloved soldiers. They found a sheltered spot away from the breeze which seemed to be moving in from the south. Janey unfolded the blanket and settled down with her book. Nora placed the basket in between some rocks and set up her easel meanwhile Brian threw down the towels lined up his soldiers on the sand and commenced building a fort. However, it was not long until he wanted to know when they were going to have their picnic.

"Now Brian, we have just arrived," said Nora in answer to his whines.

"But nan, I'm hungry!"

"Oh, go on with you, it wasn't long since you ate that big breakfast!" exclaimed his nanna.

"But I'm still hungry."

Nora took the tea towel off the basket and gave him an apple

"Here, hungry boy, have an apple. We will have our picnic in half an hour."

Brian took the apple with a disdainful look on his face as he had been hoping to have perhaps some of his nanna's fruit cake and maybe some of the delicious lemonade that he had spied a little earlier in the kitchen.

Nora daubed a few strokes onto the canvas but soon the sunshine had a soporific effect and she put down her brush and lay down on the blanket with Janey who was engrossed in her book.

"How's your tum now pet?" asked Nora.

"Not too bad nan. I think the sun is making me feel better," replied Janey shifting her position on the blanket.

"That's good darling. I thought that is what would happen. You can't beat a bit of warmth when you feel poorly. I must say the sun is making me feel rather sleepy too. I can't even be bothered painting."

Brian finishing his apple came over.

"Is it half an hour yet nan?"

"Brian, you would drive a person to drink, really you would," said Nora shielding her eyes from the sun.

Nora reached over into the basket and took out the sandwiches and the three cups into which she poured some lemonade.

Brian plonked himself down on the blanket eyes alight in anticipation of the food which would be soon making its way down into his rumbling stomach! They finished their picnic just before the clouds started creeping across the sky momentarily blotting out the sun and taking away the warmth, they were all enjoying. Nora suggested they gather up everything and head back to the house. Brian did not want to go as he was right in the middle of a full-scale battle at the sandy fort which he had constructed.

"Come on Brian." admonished Janey. "We have to go now. It's getting cold. Pick up your soldiers and help us carry everything."

Brian whinged that he just had to finish this one last battle and soldiers started flying everywhere into the sand which was becoming more soaked with the incoming tide.

"Watch out you don't get your pants wet, Brian," yelled Nora as she helped Janey fold up the blanket, and while they were wrapping up the remains of the fruit cake a wave had quickly made its way towards Brian who was now completely wet.

"Oh Brian, look at you," cried Nora when she had discovered his state.

"Come over here and let me dry you with the towel. I told you not to get wet," she cried rubbing him vigorously.

"We'll have to hurry home now and get you into some dry clothes before you catch a cold," she added.

"Sorry, nan," muttered Brian. "I didn't see the wave coming."

They hurriedly grabbed everything and made their way back up the track to the house and as soon as they got inside the wind had strengthened and big drops of rain started to fall.

"Good job we left when we did eh?" said Nora putting the basket on the table.

"Now, Brian get those wet pants off and put on some dry ones. You had better find another pullover as well, the one you have on is probably wet too."

Brian scampered up the stairs to change his clothes and Janey said she would have a lie down on her bed for a while.

"Would you like some cocoa pet?" asked Nora "I'm putting on the kettle for a cuppa."

"Yes, thanks nan I would love one," replied Janey going up to her room.

Brian passing her on the stairs asked what would she love and hearing it was cocoa immediately ran down and put his order in.

Nora had the kettle boiling on the Aga which was already warming the kitchen. She lit the fire in the sitting room as well, as she thought she might catch up on some reading. They might even have their tea there as it was cosier than sitting in the kitchen on a night such as this.

So, in front of the fire, the occupants of the little cottage sat on the sofa, dressed in their pyjamas and with mugs of pumpkin soup in their hands. They listened avidly to their favourite serial as the rain bucketed down, the Cornish wind whipping the waves into a frenzy, sending sprays of salt water up and over the cliffs of Polperro.

Chapter Nineteen

Tom had died that night. The infection which he had been battling finally had proved too much and the last words he had uttered were heard by Edward as he had been there at the final moment of his death.

"Martha, Martha" Tom had whispered as the breath of life became weaker and Edward feeling useless wished he could do more for his patient. He knew however, there was now nothing to be done, and this was the time for Tom to go. He had held his hand and when the life had been extinguished closed the eyelids and folded the pale bony hands-on top of the sheet. He had also said a prayer for Tom and for his own dear wife and all the poor souls who had died from this terrible disease. He went out of the room and located a candle in one of the cupboards then, bringing it back to Tom's room, lit it and placed it on the table. Then he went to inform the matron of Tom's passing as per the hospital protocol. He knew that before long the orderlies would arrive and transport the body to the room off the morgue where the relatives would come to view and mourn the deceased. He asked the matron if he could be the one to inform Tom's wife of his passing and as the matron did not have any problem with that he went to her office and located Martha's number. The telephone rang and rang and there was no answer. It was Friday and Martha was at Helen's minding Val while her friend had gone for tea with Mike.

It wasn't until the next morning that Martha had heard Edward telling her the news that she had been dreading. She had nearly collapsed with the shock but was aware of Edward telling her to have someone with her for support. She had staggered next door to Ethel who had gathered her in her arms and put her to bed with a cup of tea liberally dosed with sugar for the shock. She had just been able to tell Ethel Nora's number so she could let her know what had happened. Nora listened to what Martha's neighbour was saying and thanking her for conveying the tragic news went to find the children.

Janey was in the studio having another attempt at the painting she had abandoned a few days ago and Brian was there also with a brush in his hand trying to emulate his sister but only succeeding in slopping more paint on himself than on the paper.

"Ah, there you both are," said Nora walking in. "Just put your brushes down for a minute pet, I have something to tell you."

Janey and Brian put down their brushes and came over to their nanna. She put her arms around them and talked about their poor father being very sick with that disease and there was no chance of him fully recovering. She told them that he had now gone to heaven and was no longer suffering and was in a much better place now.

Janey pulled away and ran from the room. She threw herself onto her bed and wept for her poor broken da now taken from her. Now it would be just her, Brian, and ma. Oh, why was there ever a war? She would still have her da. Why did he have to go to that war? Perhaps grandma was right when she said she didn't want her Thomas to fight. She stayed there for some time until Nora knocked on the door asking if she could come in.

Janey sniffed and wiping her puffy eyes with her handkerchief told her nanna to enter. She wanted to know where her brother was and how was he coping. Nora said he was in his room playing with his soldiers. She told her that being so young the idea of his father passing probably would not have as great an impact on him as it would if he had been older. Nora said that she would bring them home on the train when she found out when the funeral was to be held.

She stroked her granddaughter's hair which now had golden highlights through it courtesy of the sun. Nora thought how she was looking more like her mother used to at her age. She had the same button nose and the smile that would light up a room. She hoped Martha would be alright and not be too sad and unable to cope without her husband. She knew how she had felt when dear Alistair had died, and she was left to bring up a child on her own.

These cruel wars, she thought always taking the lives of the men: sons, brothers, and fathers leaving mothers and their children adrift to fend for themselves. It would always be so, as long as there were greedy men in charge of making the rules.

The day of the funeral was one of torrential rain. The biting wind seeping in through the cracks of the old church's doors and windows made the assembled throng feel even colder as they knelt and prayed for the repose of Tom's soul. His coffin at the front of the church was bedecked with white and yellow daisies as Martha knew they were his favourite flowers: they reminded him of sunny days frolicking in a field with his beloved Martha beside him.

There was also an ostentatious wreath of some extravagance taking pride of place in front of the coffin: this had been sent from his mother who apparently could not attend due to her ongoing injury. However, she had been seen lunching at Claridge's only a week before albeit with a walking stick!

The message on the wreath stated –My darling son-Mother. What a hypocrite thought Martha! She did not care two hoots for him and she was glad that she was not in attendance, as she might have given her a piece of her mind funeral or not! Even Ethel had come, drowning in a cold as she looked over at her neighbour dabbing at her swollen eyes with a crumpled handkerchief.

There was another bunch of flowers on the side of the coffin. They were elegant white lilies and the message simply stated-from Millicent, Edward, and Joan. How thoughtful of them to send flowers Martha thought wiping her eyes totally unexpecting such a gesture.

As the hymn, *Nearer my God to Thee* reached its crescendo, Martha thought again how lovely it was that there had been flowers sent by them. Edward had been in touch with Martha and had told her that he had been with Tom at the minute of his death and that the last words he had uttered were her name. This has been a great comfort knowing that he had someone there with him and did not die alone, and the fact that her name was on his lips as he took his last breath was the greatest comfort of all.

She turned to look at her children: Janey, who was growing now into womanhood having commenced her monthlies and was filling out in all the places peculiar to the female form. Brian, straddling the border of a baby and a young man and looking as though he could be as tall as his father which was 6 feet 2 inches. Oh god, his father, Tom will never see them grow up, never attend any graduations, witness their marriages or hold any grandchildren in his arms, and I will be alone without my husband. This brought another bout of tears as the pallbearers carried the coffin out of the church and into the hearse to be transported to the south Ealing cemetery.

In pouring rain and buffeted by strong winds, the mourners made their way to the gravesite and gathered around while the vicar intoned the prayers for the dead. As Tom's coffin was lowered into the ground Martha had hold of Brian's hand and her arm was around Janey who was crying inconsolably. Helen, who had been able to enlist the help of the lady from the council to mind Val, was there with Mike, and, after the burial concluded, they made their way to the local pub for Tom's wake.

There was a good fire burning when they all piled through the door and, shedding their mackintoshes and umbrellas, found their seats in the snug and commenced ordering glasses of ale and lemonade for the children. There were plates of sandwiches and slices of fruit cake that Nora had made earlier and transported to the pub. She had come down with the children on the train the day after hearing the terrible news.

"So, here's to Tom," exclaimed Mike standing and raising his glass.

"To Tom," chimed in everyone else as they also raised their glasses.

"Thanks for coming Helen and Mike," said Martha sipping her ale. "It was very good of you both."

"Nonsense, what are friends for?" asked Helen as she looked at Mike and then at Martha.

"My thoughts exactly," said Mike patting Martha's hand.

Brian, eating some cake queried.

"Ma, why is everyone eating and drinking? It's like a party, da's dead and everyone should be sad."

Martha replied, "It's what happens darling after someone has died. It is called a wake or a send-off. We are giving da a good send-off on his way to heaven."

This answer seemed to satisfy Brian who then continued to have another slice of cake. Meanwhile, Janey was sitting staring into her lemonade, uncommunicative, her eyes red from crying. Martha put her arm around her shoulder hugged, her, and whispered things that would get better day by day and we will always have da in our hearts and thoughts. Nora hearing this agreed and said that time always heals the wounds and to take one day at a time.

The wake continued and, after a while, Martha and Helen decided to visit the ladies' room so, leaving Nora and Mike in charge of the children made their way there. As Martha was putting her face to rights, trying to camouflage the dark circles under her eyes with some powder that was not having the desired effect, Helen announced that she and Mike were getting along rather well, and Val seemed to be quite enamoured of him as well.

"Oh, that's excellent Helen," Martha said now trying to coax her hair into some semblance of order as the rain had made it go awry.

"We are taking everything slowly though. I don't want to rush into anything" insisted Helen as she swiped some lipstick over her lips and then pressed them together.

"No, that's sensible," said Martha. "He seems a very nice person, Helen, Tom always had a good word to say about him," and, so saying Tom's name, more tears started flowing down Martha's cheeks leaving rivulets in the fresh powder.

Helen hugged her and wiped her eyes with her handkerchief and the two friends left the ladies' room to join the others.

Chapter Twenty

The weeks went by and Martha, having been told by Helen that there was a part-time position vacant as a ward clerk at St Barts, immediately telephoned to arrange an interview. She was told to come the next day at 10:15 am so after the children had left for school, she dressed herself in her best suit which fortunately still fitted her. Then she stepped into her brown brogues and, arranging her red hat, grabbed her bag and was on her way to the bus stop for Hammersmith.

Arriving at 10:00 am, Martha found her way to the administration office and was told by the receptionist that she was early and she must wait for another 15 minutes. She sat down and opening her bag, took out her resume which she had completed the night before. She looked over it and was satisfied that all looked to be in order.

Precisely at 10:15 am she found herself in the presence of the nursing administrator who looked at Martha's proferred resume. She asked Martha how long had she been out of the workforce if she had children at home, and how old they were. Martha answered she had not worked since before her marriage and told her the ages of her children. She said that she was keen to work in a hospital environment. She enjoyed answering the telephone and was good with filing procedures. After a few minutes, she shook hands with the interviewer and was told she would be contacted when a decision would be made.

It was the next day when Martha was informed that she had been successful in securing the part-time position, and she was to commence work the following Monday. Martha was overjoyed at the prospect and thought it might help her take her mind off the loss of her darling Tom. It would occupy her time and give her something else to think about, as well as having some income to cover expenses.

As the children were getting older there seemed to be more things to buy, school excursions, clothes, and outings as well as food. It seemed to be endless. The children were quite happy for their mother to work as they knew that she would be there when they came home from school. They seemed to be less sad about their father as the days went by although there were still times when the gloom would descend as some random thing would occur to remind them of their da.

***

Monday came bringing with it a day shining with the promise of a fresh start for Martha as she boarded the bus on her way to her new job at the hospital. She sat down next to an elderly woman who sported a somewhat hairy chin.

"Mornin' dearie, goin' to work are ya?" she asked as the bus hurtled off down the road.

"Yes, actually I am. It's my first day at a new job," replied Martha giving her fare to the conductor who clipped her ticket and handed it to her.

"Oh, and where is that?" she asked.

"At St Barts hospital. I'm to be a ward clerk there."

"Is that a fact? Well, I'm goin' there an' all. Me daughter is in there. Just 'ad another kid. That'd be the sixth. She 'ad one of them cesar things."

Martha replied, "Oh, you mean a caesarean section?"

"Yer, that's the one. I told 'er to tell her Freddy to keep his pecker in his trousers from now on. They can't afford to 'ave any more of the little blighters and I can't look after them all the time they'd drive ya barmy and no mistake especially the last one she popped out, bloomin' colic, screamin' 'is lungs out I says to 'er, Violet, I says, can't ya do somethin' for this wind? Ya shouldn't have taken 'im orf the breast! And she says" ma, he'll grow out of it, a bit of cryin' don't matter. Well, I says to 'er it might be alright for you but when I'm lookin' after 'im I don't want 'im screamin' the bloomin' place down!"

She went on and on and then the bus stopped to pick up more passengers and Martha started counting the stops until she had to alight.

"You got any kids love?" she continued hardly stopping to take a breath.

"Yes, I do. A boy and a girl."

"Well, only two. Your 'ubby isn't greedy then not like that Freddy gettin' how's ya father every night!"

"Actually, I haven't a husband. He passed away recently" Martha explained wishing that her stop would arrive soon so she could extricate herself from this garrulous woman who had the rest of the passengers listening intently to the conversation.

"Oh, that's no good dearie. What he die of?"

"He had TB."

"Oh, that's a terrible thing to 'ave and no mistake. One of me uncles had it and spent a long time in that sanitary 'ouse."

"You mean the sanitarium."

"Yes, that's what I said!" she exclaimed.

Now Martha could see that she had to get off at the next stop but so also was her fellow passenger. She stood and rang the bell and headed down the stairs followed closely by the "talker".

"Now, I know a shortcut to the 'ospital, so just follow me. Me name's Aggie if ya wants to know," she said calling over her shoulder and scooting off while Martha tried to keep up.

"Oh, hello Aggie, I'm Martha," she replied breathlessly.

They arrived at the entrance after going down some sort of back alleyway which was littered with rotting garbage and numerous stray cats.

"'ere we are then. How's that for a good 'ole shortcut? Better than takin' the long way around, so'ave a good day at that job dearie. Might see ya round. Toodle loo!" she cried disappearing into the bowels of the hospital.

Martha, thankful to have some peace at last walked to the elevator which ascended to the 3rd floor where she would work. As she ascended, she thought of that ancient lift in the sanitarium which creaked and groaned, the passengers never knowing if it would arrive or not or leave them stranded in mid-flight.

Matron was there at the desk as Martha walked from the lift.

She looked up at Martha.

"Ah, you must be the new clerk?" asked the matron

"Yes, I am, how do you do?" Martha replied extending her hand.

"Now, no time for niceties I'm afraid, there is lots to do. Now put your bag down here behind the desk and I will point out the basics" the matron said shuffling the multitudinous papers which seemed to cover the desk.

As soon as Martha put down her bag the phone rang.

Matron immediately picked it up.

"Ward 17, matron speaking."

After a while, she added.

"Mrs. Jackson is only allowed to see close family members at the moment and is as well as can be expected."

She put the phone down.

"As I was saying, there is a lot to be done. Now, the girl who was here before had to be let go. As you can see, she has let things pile up. All these papers have to be filed under the patients' surname and put into the filing cabinet," she pointed to a huge cabinet against the wall.

"And," she added, "when you answer the telephone state Ward 17 and your name. What is your name by the way?"

"It's Martha, Martha Johnson."

"Very well. Now, there is a list here on the wall of the current patients on the ward. You should ensure that it is kept up to date as to the patients' condition and so on. Now, have you got all that?"

"I can't afford any more time I'm afraid," she continued. "You will have to either sink or swim, that's my motto! I have Professor Stanthorpe due in a few minutes and have to make sure the ward is top-notch. Everything in its place, professor can't abide untidiness!"

She bustled off, veil flying, to sort out the ward leaving Martha rather flummoxed as she felt overwhelmed by the number of papers in front of her. Well, nothing for it but to get started, but then the phone rang again.

"Ward 17, Martha speaking."

"Hello," said the caller. "I want to talk with Mrs. Hobbs."

Martha referred to the list and noticed there was no listing for a Hobbs, Mrs or otherwise.

"When was she admitted?" she asked.

"She was brought into the emergency yesterday."

"And to whom am I speaking?"

"It's her daughter here, Susan."

"Alright, Susan. Can you please hold the line? I have only just started working here this morning. I will have to go and ask someone about this."

Martha put Susan on hold and went to find a nurse to ask.

She located one in the sluice room rinsing out the bedpans.

"Excuse me, but I have just started working here as the clerk and I have on the phone someone asking after a Mrs. Hobbs. She doesn't appear on my list and apparently, she was admitted to the emergency department yesterday."

The nurse said.

"No, there is no one by that name on the ward. She is probably still down in the emergency and hasn't been brought up here yet."

Martha went back to the phone.

"Hello, are you there?" she asked.

"Yes, I am, and have you found my mother?"

"Well, it appears she must be still in the emergency and has not been brought up here yet. I will try to connect you to that section."

Martha connected her and hoped that the girl would be able to locate her mother then she recommenced the filing of all the patients' records. The morning seemed to fly by and soon it was time for a lunch break, but she did not know where or if there was a lunchroom. She saw the same nurse who she had asked about the missing patient, and she told her there was a tearoom at the end of the ward. She took her bag which contained some sandwiches which she had made that morning and went to track down the room. There were two nurses already there ensconced in chairs, cigarettes in hand and drinking cups of black-looking tea.

"Hello there," said Martha. "Do you mind if I sit in here to have my lunch?"

"No, to be sure," said the dark-haired one.

"Are you new here?" asked the blonde flicking the ash into a saucer.

"Yes, just started today actually," replied Martha taking the greaseproof paper off her sandwiches. "I'm Martha, the new ward clerk."

"Pleased to meet you. I'm Bernadette," said the dark one.

"And this is Jenny," pointing to the blonde who nodded and grinned.

Martha commenced eating and said, "How long have you been on the ward?"

Bernadette replied.

"We haven't been here long. We were on men's surgical for 3 months and then got transferred here. We're finding it less stressful looking after the women. Those men are cheeky buggers, with their ribald remarks and trying to pat your bottom at any opportunity!"

"Yes," chimed in Jenny. "Give some of those men an inch and they take a mile! Well, we had better get back to it otherwise we will have matron onto us like a ton of bricks. Ta ra, Martha, see you around."

They stubbed out their cigarettes and after rinsing their cups went off to another shift on the ward.

Martha finished her sandwiches and after a cup of the rather stewed tea also went back to her desk to tackle more of the paperwork which did not seem to have an end.

Chapter Twenty-One

The weeks went by and Martha had settled into her role. She got to know some of the patients who were there mainly for female complaints with the odd broken leg or arm thrown in. She also became used to the matron who, although displaying a rather officious attitude on the surface really had a good heart beating underneath. She found the nurses rather a wild bunch but as they had to deal with life and death situations. Martha understood that was their way of coping with their swearing, smoking, and sick jokes.

Bernadette, who was Irish was the funniest, as she had the Irish humour and the gift of the gab, and many a day saw Martha doubled up with laughter as she was regaled by another Irish joke. She told Martha that she was one of 14 children back in Limerick, her mother being a good catholic did not believe in taking any precautions, and her father was more often than not propping up the bar rather than working.

Her friend, Jenny, was going out with one of the interns but was having trouble with him as he was putting the hard work on her. She was in a quandary about whether she should give in to him or make him wait until she had a ring on her finger. Martha told her if he really loved her, he should control himself and agree to abide by her rules.

After a busy morning of answering the telephone and informing callers of their relatives' conditions, Martha went to update her list of patients. As she perused the names she came across a Johnson, Sylvia, Mrs. Oh no, don't say it is Tom's mother, Sylvia, it would be too much of a coincidence! She went off to find a nurse for confirmation and found Jenny making up a bed, tucking in the corners of the sheet in the manner dictated by the matron.

"Hello Jenny," said Martha holding the list of patients in her hand. "I was wondering do you know if this patient is due to be on the ward?"

Jenny looked at the name to which Martha was pointing.

"Yes, apparently, she was brought into emergency last night and is due up here soon. I am just getting the bed ready. It appears she had a fall in a convalescent home and is in rather a bad way. Do you know her at all?"

Martha, shocked to hear that it was indeed Sylvia, and she would be here in this ward said, "Yes, actually she is my mother-in-law. She broke her hip not long ago and was sent to a convalescent home for rehabilitation. I can't believe she has had another accident!"

"Well, that is a coincidence, isn't it? Tell you what, I will let you know when the orderly brings her up" said Jenny smoothing down the cover.

"Yes, thank you, I would appreciate it," replied Martha.

She went back to her desk but could not concentrate on her filing and kept turning around to see if Sylvia had been brought up. It was not long before she spied a gurney being pushed over to the bed which had been made by Jenny. She waited for a few minutes while she was installed in the bed then, after asking one of the nurses to listen for the telephone, she went over.

Sylvia's face had a deathly pallor, reminding her of darling Tom when he was close to death. Her eyes were closed, and Martha could hear a moaning sound emanating from the still form. Martha pulled a chair across and sitting down she bent over and whispered,

"Sylvia, can you hear me? It's Martha."

But there was only the sound of her rapid breathing.

Jenny came over with a syringe.

"This should make her more comfortable," she said as she plunged the injection of morphine into her arm.

"Do you know what injuries she has?" asked Martha.

"According to the report, she sustained another fracture to her hip and has a bleed on the brain. It won't be a good outcome I'm afraid, Martha, and her age doesn't help. We have noticed when an elderly person breaks a hip twice, death is not far away."

She added, "Were you close?"

Martha looked at her mother-in-law. Even though they had not gotten along she still felt sorry for the woman. She was Tom's mother after all, and a fellow human being.

"No, actually we weren't," replied Martha.

"Well, that's life, as they say. We can't get to choose our relatives," said Jenny.

"No, that's right. Well, I had better get back to my desk. If there is any change, can you let me know?"

"Sure, I will," said Jenny.

Martha went back to her desk and for the rest of the day kept looking over at her mother-in-law who lay comatose in the bed.

It was the next morning when Martha arrived at work that she was told Sylvia had passed away in the night, and the bed where she had lain was now stripped. All the bed linen had been taken to the laundry, and the body was now reposed in the morgue. Jenny went to find the matron and ask her if she could go and pay her respects.

The matron was in the middle of admonishing one of the cleaners who had missed a corner of the ward.

"This is just not good enough," she railed. "We have standards to keep in this hospital, my good man."

The unfortunate cleaner who looked like a schoolboy before the headmaster stood and incurred the matron's wrath. He sloped off to fetch the mop and bucket to clean the area he had missed.

"Excuse me, matron," said Martha when he had gone. "Could I have a word?"

Matron whirled around, the starch in her uniform crackling.

"Yes, what is it?"

"I'm sorry to interrupt matron, but you see my mother-in-law died here last night and has been taken to the morgue. I wonder if I could have permission to see her? I will ask someone to cover for me."

"Very well, I'm sorry for your loss. But make sure there is someone to answer the telephone and try not to be too long."

"Yes, I will, thank you, matron."

Martha hurried to find one of the staff to cover for her. She saw one of the voluntary women who came to change the water in the vases and bring the newspapers to the patients. She was only too pleased to answer the telephone, so Martha raced off to the elevator which would take her down to the basement where the morgue was located.

Martha walked along through the maze of gloomy corridors, the clanging water pipes above doing nothing to lighten the atmosphere. Eventually, she came to the morgue where there was an orderly sliding a body into one of the refrigerated drawers. She asked him if she could see Sylvia and she was then directed to an annex where the body lay, a sheet pulled up over the face. The orderly asked if she wanted the sheet off but Martha declined and said she would just say a prayer and then be on her way. Martha stood by Tom's dead mother and asked god to have mercy and forgive this woman her sins. She then asked for mother and son to be reconciled now in death as they were not in life.

With a heavy heart, Martha went back the way she had come through the corridors with the clanging pipes and took the elevator back to the ward. Grateful to be away from that terrible place of death, she happily answered the telephone. It continued to ring until it was time for her to go home where her children were due to arrive from school.

Chapter Twenty-Two

Sylvia was cremated as per her wishes, the urn containing the ashes deposited in the vault in which her husband's ashes also lay. Martha attended the service accompanied by Helen and Mike who were now engaged, the wedding to be held in the spring which was only a couple of months away. Martha noticed how happy Helen looked, there was a bloom on her cheeks, and she could clearly see that this dear man Mike was going to bring lots of happiness to her life. Mike was thrilled with his fiancé and said not only was he gaining a wife but also a beautiful mother-in-law whom he would help look after until god decided to take her into his keeping.

Amongst Sylvia's friends who were there in their finery, blowing air kisses to each other and calling everyone darling, there was a distinguished gentleman in a grey suit with a flamboyant bow tie around his neck. He came over to Martha and introduced himself as George Pemberthy, Sylvia's family solicitor, and then told her that there was to be a reading of the will at his office next Wednesday at 11:00 am, and would she be able to attend. Martha told him that she was working but would ask for the time off and would let him know. He produced his business card and gave it to Martha who read that his office was in Fenchurch Street, London.

On the way back from the cremation Helen, arm in arm with her precious Mike commented.

"I wonder what is in her will. The way she treated you and Tom, I can't imagine her leaving all her worldly goods to you."

"I know, it is a mystery why I have to be there unless it is a legal formality as I am in a way the next of kin."

"Well, you will find out on Wednesday. Do you think you can get the time off?" asked Helen.

"I hope so. I will have to ask matron. Maybe I can take the leave as unpaid."

Mike remarked

"Yes, that is what I would do, Marth. Just volunteer to do that. It might make things a bit easier."

They came to Helen's street and, after saying their goodbyes with promises to catch up soon, Helen and Mike walked home to spend the rest of their Saturday with Val.

Martha continued pondering about the will and what it might contain. Helen is right, she would not be leaving anything to us judging by the way she treated Tom. She stopped off at the fishmonger to buy some fish for tea. Brian and Janey were quite partial to a piece of smoked haddock, especially if it had a white sauce to accompany it.

"Three pieces of haddock please," Martha told the fishmonger.

As Martha handed over her money and receive her change a voice piped up.

"Hello Martha, I thought it was you."

Martha turned and saw that it was Edward.

"Oh, Edward, hello. How are you?"

"I'm fine thanks" he replied and in answer to the fishmonger's question "One Dover sole thank you."

Martha put the change into her purse.

Edward then said, "I was just going to have a pint at the pub before I take this back to aunts. If you're not in a hurry, would you like to join me?"

Martha is taken aback by this chance encounter did not know what to say. It might seem impolite to refuse and after all, she would have time to have one drink. Janey had gone to see a film and Brian was at a birthday party and would not be home for at least an hour.

"Oh, alright then, that would be nice. But I can't stay too long as the children will be home braying for their tea."

Edward opened the door of the shop and let Martha through.

They arrived at the pub after a short walk during which the conversation centred mainly on the coincidence of meeting at a fish shop and the state of the weather.

Edward found a vacant snug and Martha settled in as Edward went to order the drinks. A gin and tonic for her and a pint for him.

"Here we are," said Edward as he set their glasses on the table.

"Thank you," said Martha taking a sip.

"Well, it's good to see you again Martha. I was terribly sorry about Tom, well we all were actually, mother and aunt."

"Yes, I appreciated everything you did for him, Edward, being there at the end. It really meant a lot to me knowing he did not die on his own. And also thank you all for sending the beautiful lilies, it was most thoughtful."

Edward fingered his glass.

"Oh, that's alright. Mother thought it was appropriate. She told me she thought you were lovely."

Martha blushed.

"It was very generous of her to take me in that day and let me stay the night. I was rather embarrassed about the whole situation, but she really put me at ease. Are you staying with your aunt at the moment?"

"Yes, just for the weekend. She's a twitcher and went away to one of the events they hold every so often."

Martha looked puzzled.

"A twitcher?"

"Yes, a bird watcher, it's really called ornithology. My uncle used to be an enthusiast and when he died, my aunt developed an interest also. It keeps her amused and gives her something to do. I usually come and feed her cat when she's away."

He took a sip of ale.

"Oh, I see. Well, as long as she enjoys it. What sort of cat has she?" Martha asked.

"He's just a tabby, nothing exotic, but he certainly lets one know when he wants his food. Scratches at the bedroom door at 5 am and keeps it up until someone comes and fills up his food bowl."

"Oh, he sounds like a crying baby" exclaimed Martha stirring the lime around in her drink with the straw.

"Yes, that is a good example" laughed Edward.

Martha looked at her watch and noticed the time.

"Sorry Edward, but it looks like it's time for me to go. Thanks for the drink. It was lovely to catch up with you."

Edward stood up and finished the last of his ale. He went ahead and opened the door to let Martha through.

"Well, thanks for your company," he said.

"I say," he added. "If it isn't too forward, and if you and the children are free tomorrow, I wonder if you might like to go to the zoo. I was going anyway. There is an elephant that has just been born which would be worth a look. I must confess I rather like the zoo. Suppose I am just a big kid at heart."

Martha found herself accepting his offer. She knew tomorrow was going to be quiet and there was something about Sundays that made her feel a bit depressed, especially these days now that Tom was not around to keep her company.

They arranged to meet at the entrance to the zoo at 11 am and then they went their separate ways, each carrying the fish which they had purchased about an hour before.

Janey and Brian were pleased with the prospect of visiting the zoo, especially Brian who loved seeing the animals: in particular, the alpacas which he had been learning about at school. They reminded him of poor Lucy who he secretly missed sometimes in the hours of darkness when in bed his thoughts would stray to the time when he and the goat fell over the cliff. Then he would find himself crying into his pillow, trying not to disturb his sister and ma who he knew would worry about him and make a fuss. No, it was best that he kept such thoughts between him and his pillow.

The outing to the zoo was a big success. Edward took them to the cafe where they consumed bacon and egg sandwiches. Afterward, near the elephant enclosure where they all were in raptures over the new baby elephant, he bought them strawberry ice creams which Brian devoured with relish.

As the day progressed with Janey taking charge of Brian, Martha and Edward found themselves conversing about various topics with a sense of ease and familiarity which surprised them both.

He told her a little of his life. At the lion enclosure, he explained that his father had been quite domineering, and he was pressured into studying for a medical degree at Cambridge which had been his father's alma mater, and he was expected to keep up the family tradition. He told her that he always felt like he was never good enough or would never be able to achieve the success that his father had, having been appointed a professor at the age of 39 and been included in The Royal College of Surgeons thereafter.

Martha had listened and had found herself feeling sorry for this man whose life was sounding a lot like her dear Tom's albeit with a domineering mother, pressuring him to study at university when it was not the life that he had wanted for himself.

Whilst entertained by the antics of the apes, Martha told him of her childhood growing up in Cornwall without a father but a loving mother more than making up for it. Edward said that he had fond memories of Cornwall as his maternal grandparents had lived at Penzance. Many school holidays had been spent there, either at the beach when it was hot, or on the moors in the cooler weather.

Martha could not believe that they had so much in common and at the end of what had been a glorious day, she had told him about her deceased mother-in-law, and that she had to attend the reading of her will that week. They had then determined they would stay in touch with each other as Edward had escorted them back to Uxbridge Road.

Chapter Twenty-Three

At exactly 11 am on Wednesday 28th March, at 54 Fenchurch Street, London, in the office of George Pemberthy solicitor, Martha found herself in the company of another formidable-looking person sartorially splendid in a grey pin-stripe suit and blue tie, who was introduced as Nigel Livingstone, curator of the British National Art Gallery. They were offered tea which was eventually delivered by the ancient phlegmatic secretary who shuffled in with the tray. Plonking it down on the mahogany desk she shuffled off to the consternation of Pemberthy who seemed rather embarrassed about the whole event.

After they had drunk their tea which the secretary had managed to spill into the saucers, they discussed mundane matters such as the weather and the progress of the restoration of the bombed-out buildings in the city. Then Pemberthy cleared his throat and announced it was time for the formal reading of the will.

He commenced that they were here today for the reading of the last will and testament of Sylvia Winifred Johnson formerly of 2 Belgrave Square, Belgravia in the city of London. He continued that she revokes all other wills and testaments and that this is her only legal will.

"I appoint my solicitor George Winston Pemberthy to be the executor and trustee of this my will."

He cleared his throat again and announced.

"I give devise and bequeath my estate, wheresoever situate free of all taxes and death duties to the National Gallery of London."

Martha, transfixed and shocked by this revelation looked across at Livingstone who was stroking his tie and licking his lips, mentally calculating how many works of art and artifacts the Gallery could purchase with a windfall such as this!

Helen was right, of course, she was never going to leave the family anything, what was she doing, she should be at work earning some money, not sitting here wasting time!

"And to my granddaughter," Pemberthy droned on. "Janey Ann Johnson, I leave Dawn After the Wreck by Joseph Mallord William Turner free of all taxes and death duties for her sole use and benefit.

Martha's heart seemed to stop beating. She left the Turner to Janey! Darling Janey! She did leave us something! Now it was Martha's turn to mentally calculate the worth of such a painting. My god, an original Turner, it was unbelievable! Looking back, Martha remembered her mother-in-law over the years seemed to have shown some sort of interest in Janey, and maybe she had looked upon her as her substitute daughter not having had one of her own.

Maybe because she had learnt of Janey's burgeoning talent in art, Martha had told her of Janey's enrolment in an after-school art class, and that she had bequeathed to her this famous painting. Perhaps we will never know her reasons, people were certainly a mystery, and no one could ever read what was in someone's mind no matter how close we are to them.

Pemberthy droned on, Martha being only half aware of what else he was saying. Something about the payment of funeral expenses, where the ashes were to be deposited, standard provisions, and the attestation.

The meeting concluded and Martha shook hands with the two gentlemen, Pemberthy telling her that he would be in touch regarding the transportation of the picture which was expected to occur within the month.

It was as though in a dream that Martha sat on the bus to return to work at the hospital. She felt like taking the rest of the day off and repairing to the Ritz for a sumptuous dinner washed down with a bottle of Moet, all brought by a bevy of waiters! However, she was soon brought out of her reverie.

"Oi, 'ow are ya love?" said the familiar voice.

"Thought it was you."

Oh no, thought Martha, don't tell me it's that woman who bailed me up on my first day at work!

"Oh, hello," said Martha.

She sat down next to Martha.

"Well, fancy meetin' you again," she hollered. "Been somewhere has ya?"

"Yes, actually I've been to see a solicitor."

"Oh, in trouble are ya lovie?"

"Oh no, nothing like that" Martha replied wishing that she would leave her alone to wallow in her dreams.

"What did ya have to see him for then?"

"I had to attend a reading of a will."

"Ooh, and did ya get some dough left to ya?" she smirked giving Martha a poke in the arm with her bony elbow.

"As a matter of fact, my daughter had something left to her," Martha replied not wanting to go into any more detail but the woman was not to be stopped.

"What was it?"

"It was a painting by a famous artist."

"Well, good for 'er then, eh? She can sell it 'orf and have the life of Riley. That's what I'd be doin' and no mistake, paintin' the town red!"

Martha could not be bothered telling the woman that her daughter was only 12 and thankfully it was now time for her to get off the bus.

"Toodle loo," yelled the woman through the window as Martha alighted. "' Ope ya daughter lives it up with all that loot!"

Martha, squirming with embarrassment, walked on to the hospital where the matron was waiting to accost her about all the unfinished tasks she had to complete before she went home at 3 pm.

Martha threw her bag behind her desk and commenced to sort through the paperwork which had grown considerably from when she had left this morning. She did not have time to stop for a lunch break and the sandwiches which she had packed that morning were left to dry out in her bag.

After making some headway into the filing, she dialled Nora's number to apprise her of the good news, as she thought she would burst if she did not tell someone soon.

"Mum," she whispered, "It's me, Martha."

"Oh darling, how are you? I was just thinking of you, must have been telepathy."

"Mum, I'm ringing from work and can't stay long. I just wanted to tell you that Sylvia left the Turner painting to Janey!"

"What?" exclaimed her mother. "The Turner, Dawn After the Wreck?"

"Yes, that's the one!"

Oh, Martha, I can't believe it. You know when Janey was here, she mentioned that she liked that painting. Oh, but that's wonderful!"

"Yes, I know, I can hardly believe it. Of course, she left the estate to the National Gallery." Martha continued whispering.

"Well, we all thought as much, didn't we?"

"Yes. Mum, I have to go now. Matron is coming. Talk to you soon."

Martha hung up the telephone just as matron bustled up to the desk.

"Everything under control now Martha?" she said looking at the papers which had now diminished considerably since the last time she was there.

"Oh yes, matron. I think I have broken the back of it."

"Very good," said the matron.

She hurried down the ward straightening her veil as she went, and Martha continued, answering the calls of distressed relatives and filing the patients' records. Then it was time to leave for home where the good news would be relayed to Janey and Brian and all her closest friends.

Chapter Twenty-Four

As the weeks went by, the British postal and telephone services assisted Martha and Edward in furthering their relationship, as letters flew back and forth interspersed with telephone calls. There were odd weekends when Edward invited Martha and the children to his house at Frimley. Edward would cook them his specialty which was roast beef and Yorkshire pudding, the recipe having been handed down from his grandmother to his mother and thence to Edward.

Martha would be given Edward's bed, while he would content himself on the sofa while the children would share the spare bedroom, much to the chagrin of Janey, who told her mother she needed some privacy away from Brian.

This problem had been alleviated by the loan of a camp bed from one of Edward's mates and Edward had set it up for Brian in the corner of the sitting room telling him that he could pretend to be camping out in the jungle. This seemed to ameliorate the situation and soon peace was restored between brother and sister.

Sometimes on the nights when Edward manifested his culinary skills, his mother would come to tea, occasionally to be joined by her husband who, upon meeting Martha for the first time, displayed quite a hubristic attitude towards her.

She could sense that his and Millicent's marriage was not a happy one as he disparaged her at every opportunity. Martha could now see why Millicent had commented the night she had stayed about enjoying the times when her husband was away and making egg and toast soldiers for herself.

She wondered why Millicent stayed with this man who was clearly making her life unhappy, constantly being psychologically abused. She said as much to Edward when there was a quiet moment one night after his parents had left and the children were ensconced in their books. The dinner had nearly been ruined as Millicent, after another snide remark had been made by her husband, had left the table in floods of tears.

"I know, Martha, I have suggested it to her, but she is from the old school and thinks there is a stigma attached to divorce," Edward had said as he let the washing-up water drain down the sink.

"And," he added, "apart from which father would never agree to it."

Martha took a plate and wiped it with the tea towel.

"It just seems a shame," she replied. "Your mother is so lovely and shouldn't be treated like that, and you can see that they are clearly both unhappy."

When Martha retired that night, sleep had eluded her for quite some time as her thoughts flew to poor Millicent trapped in a loveless marriage and not having the courage to leave it.

Edward waved them off at the station the next day where they boarded the 3 pm express to Ealing Broadway.

"Bye, thank you for another beautiful weekend, Edward," said Martha leaning out the door.

"Glad you enjoyed it," replied Edward kissing her on the cheek.

Brian and Janey both chorused their thanks and Brian asked if he could always sleep on the camp bed when he came to stay.

"Of course, you can young man" replied Edward smiling "You have to keep those natives from attacking us in the night!"

"I'll ring you when we have arrived," Martha said as the door was closing. "And don't forget about the wedding."

Edward stayed until the train could no longer be seen and then he made his way back to the house where he took the sheets off the camp bed. Folding it up he put it away under the stairs ready to be assembled when Brian visited again. Then he took the sheets off the sofa, Janey's bed, and his bed where Martha had slept.

Darling Martha, he thought as he sniffed the sheet on which she had lain. I think I am falling in love with you, but dare I tell you? Am I ready to commit to another marriage? Will you also die like Nicky did and leave me desolate and sorrowful? Will my marriage turn out like my parents with no love existing only unhappiness and wretchedness? And then where would we all live? Do I want to continue at the sanitarium or strike out on my own as a GP somewhere? Would Martha want to continue living in Ealing?

These thoughts continued until pouring himself a glass of wine and putting on Wagner's Ride of the Valkyries he finally settled into his armchair determined to broach some of these subjects when next he saw his beloved Martha.

Chapter Twenty-Five

On a beautiful spring day on the 14th of April 1947 at 11 am Helen and Mike stood at the altar in St Mary's church Ealing and exchanged their marriage vows. Martha, the maid of honour, dressed in a taffeta pale green dress, holding Helen's bouquet of forsythia and baby's breath was aware of a moistening in her eyes as Mike placed the ring on her friend's finger.

She had confided in Martha that Mike had said there was not going to be any pressure to have their marriage consummated, as he was aware of the terrible trauma she had experienced in her childhood. That was quite a relief for poor Helen, as she had told Martha she had not been looking forward to that side of things and was hesitant to mention it to Mike.

Having pride of place in the front of the pew, was a smart wheelchair in which Val sat, Mike, having organised that and the lady from the council to accompany her for the day. With her hair freshly washed and curled for the occasion, and dressed in a newly purchased gown, she watched with pride as her only daughter and Mike were proclaimed husband and wife. Edward stood with Janey and Brian, Janey completely absorbed in the ceremony and visualising how it would look painted on canvas!

As the ceremony continued, Martha found herself thinking of Edward who was standing in the first pew with Janey and Brian. The night before the wedding, while Janey minded Brian, he had taken her to tea, or dinner as he called it.

Over candlelight, Dover sole, and a bottle of Lafite, he had spoken of his feelings for her and the children. He told her of his hesitancy towards marriage, his outlook coloured by his personal experiences, and his ambivalence towards his career as a doctor in the wards of the sanitarium.

Martha had listened to this dear man with whom she wanted to be. She was also concerned about him taking the place of her Tom and taking the place of her children's father. They both agreed they would take one day at a time until they were certain of their feelings for each other.

Nora had come from Polperro for the wedding and she and Martha had also discussed what the future held for them all. She told her mother of the relationship she had with Edward and her thoughts of moving away from Ealing as it held too many bad memories for her. Nora advised that her daughter and Edward stay good friends until they both were certain of a future together. In the meantime, she suggested that Martha and the children move in with her. They agreed that the Turner would be sold with part of the money going towards adding an extra room to the cottage. Nora had intended to do that one day, and now there were extra funds, she could proceed with the renovation. The rest of the money would be put into trust for the children when they came of age, with, of course, a little something to be shared between Nora and her daughter!

Nora told Martha that there were now quite good schools in Cornwall, and there was also an art school due to open in a few months where Janey could enrol. So, to the delight of Janey and Brian, they all went to live with their beloved nanna and her pets on top of the cliff in Polperro.

Chapter Twenty-Six

"They were beautifully behaved," Martha exclaimed to Helen.

They were all leaving the church after the christening of Helen's and Mike's twin girls who had been born prematurely but were now the picture of health.

"Yes," replied Mike. "I thought one would start screaming and then set the other off as always seems to happen."

"Val would have been so proud," said Martha.

Dear Val had lived for only a short time after Helen and Mike's marriage. She slipped away quietly in her sleep after Mike had read to her the third chapter of Jane Austen's, Emma

After deciding that they would move to Cornwall, Martha had left St Barts and the matron, quite saddened by her resignation had organised a small farewell. The tearoom had been bursting at the seams with all the nurses and orderlies who dropped in to say goodbye, have some cake and wish Martha all the best.

It was not long after they moved that Edward's father died suddenly from a massive coronary occlusion. He had been found conjoined with his paramour, his penis stuck fast and she unable to extricate herself, had just managed to ring for help. The two lovers one dead and the other alive, highly hysterical, had then been taken on a stretcher to Westminster hospital, where they had been prised apart. It had taken weeks for the gossip in the hospital to subside, however, at the private clubs and dinner parties of the medical fraternity conversations inevitably turned to Charles Young's infamous demise!

Millicent subsequently decided to embark on an overseas holiday on the advice of her son and invited Joan to accompany her. Hearing of this, Mike, through his work, had been able to secure two discounted tickets on the Aquitania, one of the Cunard liners. It was leaving from Southhampton stopping at Cherbourg en route to New York. They decided they would travel a few weeks before the ship was due at Cherbourg where they would embark. They would travel firstly to Italy and then to France, in particular Normandy, to visit the graves of their dead sons.

The first stop was Sicily, where Millicent indulged her new-found interest in Italian food, in particular, spaghetti alle vongole. She planned to introduce the daily to some of the recipes as she was tired of the same bland English fare, the Italian food was so much more flavoursome she found! Meanwhile, Joan had discovered that there was good bird watching to be had here, the Lanner population being the biggest in Europe. There were said to be 100-120 pairs!

On a perfect sunny day, binoculars in hand, Joan enjoined with the other enthusiastic twitchers, albeit Italian, who were all vying to spot the rare Bonelli's eagle which was declining in Sicily. Although Joan was unable to speak Italian, she found that twitching did not require much communication. The hand gestures and finger pointing seemed to be enough indication when a bird was sighted, and she soon was familiar with the word "guarda" which was Italian for "look!"

Then to Normandy where the sisters visited the graves of Jeffrey and Nevil who were buried at the Bayeux British military cemetery. There they both mourned and prayed for their sons who had given their lives for their country. They left flowers and their tears mingled with the green grass of this their boys' final resting place in France.

After a few more days of indulging in croissants, cafe au lait, and sampling exotic delicacies such as escargots and frogs' legs, it was time for Joan and Martha to board the train. They were leaving Normandy for Cherbourg where their ship awaited to take them across the seas to New York!

Ah, New York! The city that never sleeps! Here they were in Times Square no less after a smooth crossing with not a sign of sea sickness between them. They thoroughly enjoyed life on the high seas and had dined at the captain's table on several occasions. Millicent had found herself rarely without a partner at the après dinner dances which occurred every night. Joan was content to sit and converse with other like-minded people as she watched her sister being whirled around the floor by numerous tuxedoed partners.

"Milly," exclaimed Joan. "I can't believe we are actually in New York!"

"Yes, isn't it marvellous! How about after luncheon we go to the top of the Empire State building?"

"Ooh, yes, let's. I have always wanted to go there. But I hope I don't get vertigo! Apparently, it is rather high at the top!"

The elevator deposited them and other tourists at the top of the tallest building in the world where they were in complete awe of the view. They took photos of each other and bought coffees then descended in the elevator back to 34th street where they were once again caught up in the milling throng.

"Well, that was certainly worth it, I must say," said Millicent as she adjusted her hat which had been knocked sideways by a man hurrying past with a large dog on a lead.

"Yes, wasn't it?" replied her sister. "And the vertigo was not too bad either, thank goodness."

They decided that after such a busy time they would go back to their hotel, the Roosevelt, to have a rest before deciding where they would dine later. Joan heard the Oyster Bar and Restaurant in Grand Central Station was highly recommended, but Millicent wanted some Italian cuisine. They compromised by going to Joan's recommendation tonight and tomorrow Luigi's on 64th street would be the venue.

The sisters were not disappointed as both restaurants lived up to their reputations: the freshly shucked oysters with lemon were voted the best they had tasted and the veal scallopine at Luigi's washed down with a bottle of Chianti had been according to Millicent, delizioso!

"I'm so glad the concierge obtained the tickets," said Joan. "It looks like it will be a full house."

They were now at the Royale Theatre on Broadway about to see *The Importance of Being Earnest* which they had heard had good reviews.

"Yes," replied her sister. "That hotel certainly looks after one. Nothing is too much trouble for them."

"That's right Milly. And everything in walking distance," replied Joan taking her program and leafing through it.

The curtain was raised, a hush came over the audience and the sisters sat entranced as the play began.

"Well, that was marvellous!" exclaimed Millicent after the final curtain call, their hands tired from the applause.

"I do love Margaret Rutherford. She played Bracknell so well, didn't she?" asked Joan. "Oh yes," responded Millicent "But Gielgud is my favourite. He is always so debonair."

They joined the rest of the audience spilling out into the New York night and decided that as it was their last evening, they would have a nightcap at one of the bars back at the Roosevelt.

Ensconced in a plush leather banquette with a view of the passing parade of after-dark revellers, the sisters toasted each other with dry martinis.

"Here's to us then," said Joan as she clinked her glass against Millicent's.

"Yes, to us," replied Millicent smiling.

She took a sip.

"I must say they do a good martini here Joan. Just the way I like it. Nice and dry!"

Joan agreed and bit the olive off the toothpick.

"We have had a wonderful time Milly," she said. "I hope puss did not fret too much in that cattery. He's never had to go to one before. Edward had always been able to mind him."

"I'm sure he has been fine Joan. He has probably had the time of his life and met a girlfriend or two," joked Millicent.

Joan fingered her drink.

"Do you think you will ever come back here Milly?"

"Well," Millicent replied. "I might, but I really enjoyed Italy. I think I would love to return and see some more of that country. The little villages for instance, and Tuscany."

As they sipped their martinis, they discussed Edward and Martha.

"I do think they are suited to each other," Joan said. "And I really like Martha."

"Oh yes, she is a sweet thing. I took to her that first day I met her when she became ill at the sanitarium. I do hope they can work things out."

She added.

"I think poor Edward's attitude towards marriage has been coloured somewhat by his father's and mine," she looked towards the window. "The poor boy has been witness to a lot of unpleasant things when he was growing up: I can't forget the eye I had when he was fourteen-it was blue for a week. And to die like that!"

Joan put her hand on her sister's and patting it said, "That's all in the past now dear. Chin up. Now, what say we have another one of those dry martinis before we retire to our beds for our last night in the Big Apple?"

The next morning to the sound of a band playing, *Anchors Aweigh* and with streamers raining down on the waving crowd, the Aquitania slowly left the dock at New York harbour. With their arms around each other, the sisters stood on the deck and as the skyscrapers became smaller and smaller, they knew they were on their way back home to England.

Chapter Twenty-Seven

As Martha sat in front of a crackling fire, the strains of Wagner filling the room, a brandy in hand, she ruminated about life. How she had been raised solely by her mother now in spirit: her ashes taken to the Scilly Isles spread on the water on which she had sailed with Alistair. The terrible time trying to abort her baby and ending up in that horrendous unmarried mother's home: her baby given away to strangers. She thought of the traumatic childhood of Helen, now happily married to Mike, and them being the doting parents of twins.

Now Martha was married to Edward as they had sorted out their differences and came to the conclusion that they could not live apart any longer. They were betrothed at Aldourie Castle near Inverness in Scotland. The laird who had owned it was a family friend of Millicent's and by sheer coincidence was a very distant relative of Alistair.

Dressed in a fine wool crepe beige suit and matching hat, Martha had been escorted and given to Edward by Mike. They had been followed by Janey who had looked quite the young lady, her hair swept up into a knot encircled with flowers. Then, holding a tiny cushion on which sat two rings, Brian, head down and walking carefully, had followed his sister to join the rest of the wedding party. To the overture of bagpipes, the happy couple had walked outside the castle, showered with confetti, and posed for the obligatory photographs with their families and close friends.

Ethel was among the well-wishers and, to the surprise of everyone, had introduced her bald escort as Harry, her fiancé, the bingo caller. They were to marry and planned to move to Skegness. Harry had a better job lined up in the holiday camp there and would be earning much more than he was now. Ethel had also said that 79 Uxbridge Road was now occupied by Indians. The smells of turmeric and saffron which seeped through the walls had her thinking she was living next to the local curry house and no mistake! Her moving day could not come quickly enough!

The day after the wedding, Nora had taken the children back with her leaving Martha and Edward to enjoy their honeymoon at the Scottish castle albeit for a few days. The glens and deer were witness to their stolen kisses as they rambled over the heather, a picnic basket packed by the chef in Edward's hand. Plodda falls was their destination and, after reaching the wondrous site, they had lain on their rug, all thoughts of the picnic banished, as the thunderous waterfall obliterated their cries of passion.

Edward had resigned from the sanitarium and had secured a post as the local doctor in St Ives. Martha had become his receptionist and she had heard that more women patients were coming to the surgery than when old Dr. Watkins used to work there. Apparently, they were coming to see that handsome new doctor who had taken over the practice!

As she drained the last of the brandy, she thought of meeting Tom and having his children, and the worry about him in the war and in the camp. Of his contracting TB and dying in that sanitarium which was where she had met Edward. She thought Tom would have approved of this man who had proved to be a devoted father and a loving husband. He also would have been proud of his children: Janey, who was establishing a reputation as a talented artist, holding exhibitions in the boutique galleries of London, and Brian, who had bought acreage in Devon and was happily raising a herd of angora goats. Nora's cottage had ultimately been sold after a family conference had made the decision. There was now a family living there who apparently loved the place and the animals as much as they had.

Her mind turned to Millicent, who was now enjoying life after suffering years of abuse from her husband. Firstly, she went on that wonderful holiday with her sister. Then returning, she learnt some Italian from an elderly Nonna who had wanted to earn some extra money. Now Millicent was conducting gourmet tours to Tuscany and loving every minute of it!

"A penny for your thoughts, darling," Edward said as he put down the book he was reading, turned, and kissed her head.

"Oh, I was just thinking about the journey of life," she said looking into the fire and fingering her glass.

"The way we travel through, the good times and the bad, the ups and the downs, and I do think there have to be bad times, otherwise we do not appreciate the good."

"Well, that's quite percipient of you, I must say!"

"You and your long words!" Martha retorted smiling.

Edward took her glass.

"Another brandy?"

"Oh, yes please, that would be lovely!"

Martha leaned back into the sofa as her husband went to replenish their drinks.

"Here we are then," he said handing Martha the glass. "Just what the doctor ordered, cheers."

"Cheers," she replied.

As the soggy night clamped firmly down on the house, and the shrieking wind whipped the sea into a frenzy, sending spray up against the cliff, Martha and Edward clinked glasses and snuggled together for a cosy night in front of the fire.

THE END

The following helped me in my research for my book:
If this is a Woman: Inside Ravensbruck by Yvonne Roberts
Extracts from the diary of a woman TB patient in 1944 in the Journal of the Royal Society of Medicine.

About the Author

From an early age, Annette was encouraged to write and was awarded several prizes for English.

A native of Sydney, Australia, she published a short story at the age of twelve.

She remained passionate about her writing, but the demands of raising a family left no time for writing.

Now retired, Annette has reignited her passion and has written six books with the seventh nearing completion.

Her interest lies in novels set around the periods of the first and second world wars.

Annette lives with her partner, Stephen, at Neutral Bay, a suburb on Sydney harbor in Australia. She has two sons, Mark and Brett, two grandsons, Jaime and Flynn, and a sister, Maree.

79 UXBRIDGE ROAD is her fourth published novel.